FULL-COURT PRESS
BOOK 2

Other books in the
Spirit of the Game series

FULL-COURT PRESS

BOOK 2

BY TODD HAFER

ZONDERVAN™

GRAND RAPIDS, MICHIGAN 49530 USA

ZONDERVAN.COM/
AUTHORTRACKER

This book is dedicated to the life and memory
of Tim Hanson, a true athlete, a true friend.

ZONDERVAN™

Full-Court Press
Copyright © 2004 by Todd Hafer

Requests for information should be addressed to:
Zondervan, Grand Rapids, Michigan 49530

Library of Congress Cataloging-in-Publication Data

Hafer, Todd.
   Full-court press / Todd Hafer.– 1st ed.
      p. cm. — (The spirit of the game sports fiction series)
   Summary: An eighth-grade basketball player finds his training, both
physical and spiritual, put to the test too soon after his mother's death.
   ISBN-10: 0-310-70668-8 (softcover)
   ISBN-13: 978-0-310-70668-7 (softcover)
   [1. Basketball —Fiction. 2. Grief—Fiction. 3. Christian life—Fiction.]
I. Title. II. Series.
   PZ7.H11975Fu 2005
   [Fic]--dc22   2004000186

Editor: Bruce Nuffer
Cover design by Alan Close
Interior design: Susan Ambs
Art direction: Laura Maitner
Photos by Synergy Photographic
Printed in the United States of America

06 07 08 09 10 11 12 • 10 9 8 7 6 5 4 3

Contents

Foreword

I love sports. I have always loved sports. I have competed in various sports at various levels, right through college. And today, even though my official competitive days are behind me, you can still find me on the golf course, working on my game, or on a basketball court, playing a game of pick-up.

Sports have also helped me learn some of life's important lessons–lessons about humility, risk, dedication, teamwork, friendship. Cody Martin, the central character in "The Spirit of the Game" series, learns these lessons too. Some of them, the hard way. I think you'll enjoy following Cody in his athletic endeavors.

Like most of us, he doesn't win every game or every race. He's not the best athlete in his school, not by a long shot. But he does taste victory, because, as you'll see, he comes to understand that life's greatest victories aren't reflected on a scoreboard. They are the times when you rely on a strength beyond your own —a spiritual strength—to carry you through. They are the times when you put the needs of someone else before your own. They are the times when sports become a way to celebrate the life God has given you.

So read on, and may you always possess the true Spirit of the Game.

Toby McKeehan

Chapter 1
Trial and Air

"It's time to attempt suicide!" barked Coach Clayton.

"Everyone on the line!"

"Aww—I hate suicides," Alston groaned. Cody looked at the star point guard, who was bent over beside him, hands on his knees. Terry Alston's neck gleamed with perspiration. The back of his sweat-soaked gray practice T-shirt clung tightly to his back. Cody studied the sweat stain, noting that its shape looked like the continent of Africa.

"Here's the deal," Coach Clayton said with a smile. "Whoever wins the first suicide gets to shower. The rest of you—ah, I pity the rest of you. Because I'm going to work you like government mules. Now, let's see who's quick enough to escape the pain."

"The first day of tryouts wasn't like this last year," Alston whispered. "This new coach—I don't like him."

"I heard he coached at Holmes last year." said Pork Chop, who, sitting to Cody's left, was frantically lacing up a size-ten Nike. "I saw him shooting before practice. He's got game."

"Whatever," Alston snorted. "And don't worry about your shoelaces, Chop. You're not gonna win this suicide anyway. It takes you too long to get all of that beef moving."

"You never know," Pork Chop replied, smiling grimly. "When I get all this beef moving, the momentum is something to behold. I might win. Even Cody here might take it. At least neither of us smokes Marlboros, like you do."

Alston arched his eyebrows. "Martin? Win? He's got no wheels. Do you, Martin?"

Cody stared at his worn-out Adidas. He felt anger rising inside him. Then he thought of the words his youth pastor, Blake Randall, spoke on Sunday— "When words are many, sin is not absent."

Cody felt too tired to say anything sinful, but he decided it was best to take no chances. He stared straight ahead and stayed silent.

Pork Chop finished double-lacing his shoe and rose slowly to his feet.

"Well," said Pork Chop, "they say this Colorado air is thinner than in other places. That ought to give us nonsmokers an edge."

Instantly, Coach Clayton blew a shrill blast on his whistle. Alston swore under his breath and exploded off the baseline at the south end of the court.

Alston had the fastest feet Cody had ever seen. He touched the near free throw line with his left foot, then changed direction like a ricochet. He reached the south end line again—two strides ahead of Cody—then sprinted for half court. Cody struggled to keep up. He stayed low, he ran straight, and he didn't look around. He focused on each line. The squeaking shoes, panting, and occasional swearing swirled around him in another dimension.

He wasn't gaining any ground on Alston, but he wasn't losing any either. On the long last sprint, from end line to end line, Alston slowed noticeably. *Must be the cigarettes*, Cody thought. He pumped his arms furiously and focused on driving his knees forward. As he crossed half court, he was only a step behind Alston. Cody lengthened his stride, straining to devour the distance between himself and the fastest athlete in the school.

As they hit the south free throw line, Cody saw Alston glance over his shoulder. They were almost stride for stride now. As they crossed the end line, Alston's track experience saved him. He leaned forward, edging Cody by inches. Victorious, Alston slammed into the slice of crimson wrestling mat that hung on the wall under the basket. Then he slumped to the floor and coughed like a barking seal.

Cody kicked the wall in disgust. Pork Chop finished third, two strides behind Cody. He sunk to his hands and knees, his caramel skin wet with sweat, and began panting as if he were trying to blow out birthday candles—lots of them.

Meanwhile, Alston had staggered to the gym's south doors. He stood under the green exit sign, smiling. "Have a nice run, boys!" he laughed before erupting into another coughing fit.

Coach Clayton glared at Alston. "I suggest you shut up, Slick. Save your air. And I suggest you learn to do without the cigarettes this season. I don't allow 'em."

Alston gave the coach a startled look, then exited the gym as if it were on fire.

Pork Chop shook his head. "Man, how does Coach know Alston smokes? Does he have ESP or something?"

"How many eighth graders cough like coal miners?" Cody asked.

"Alston's been smoking since he was twelve," noted Brett Evans, the better of the Evans twins—although both had made the starting five the previous season.

"It's not fair that he won," Bart Evans said. "He cheats. He never touches all the lines!"

Coach Clayton's whistle pierced Cody's eardrums again. As he planted his foot on the free throw line, he felt a blister forming on his right instep. He tried to keep his weight on the outside of his foot, but then his calf started to cramp. He finished suicide number two just behind Brett. Pork Chop was third again.

Midway through the third suicide, Cody felt the chili-dog and thirty-two-ounce soda he had for lunch rising in his throat. He finished running, dropping to fourth place this time, then dashed from the gym, through the small foyer between the gym and the locker room. Once outside, he doubled over and relinquished his lunch on a knee-high pile of snow that had been cleared from the entryway at the school's south end.

He straightened and watched his breath vaporize in front of his face as he exhaled heavily. His throat burned, and his stomach muscles ached, as if he had been gut-punched. He turned and jogged back to the gym.

Coach Clayton smiled as Cody toed the line again. "Lose your lunch, Martin?"

"Oh, I bet he didn't lose it, Coach," Pork Chop said. "I bet he knows right where it is."

Cody thought he was too spent to smile, but he felt an almost involuntary tugging at the corners of his mouth.

"I'll tell you what," Coach Clayton said, "if you all will make this one count—really bust it—we're done, okay? But if I see even one guy dogging it, you'll keep running. I don't care if we go all night."

Cody inhaled hungrily. "One more," he said quietly to no one in particular. He heard the whistle and willed his feet to move. He concentrated on braking with his left foot. He knew he had opened the blister on his right and guessed it was the size of a quarter at least.

As Cody headed for the far end line, he felt someone pull alongside him. It was Coach Clayton. "Martin!" The voice blasted in Cody's ear. "There are fifteen seconds left in the game! We're down by one! If you get downcourt quickly enough, you can get the inbound pass and score a layup! Come on—the ball's in the air! Sprint for it, or it'll go out of bounds!"

Cody pumped his arms and churned his legs. His quadricep muscles burned with fatigue, but he matched the loose-limbed coach stride for stride. They touched the end line together. Cody winced as he made a half turn and pushed off with his right foot. *Just one more court length to go.*

"Good, Martin—you got the layup," Coach said. "But there are still five seconds left. Now the other team has the ball. The opposing point guard is streaking downcourt. He's ahead of you. You gotta catch him and steal the ball, or it's an easy bucket and we lose. You gotta save the game!"

Cody saw Brett three strides ahead of him as they crossed the north free throw line. He pretended he saw Macy instead. Loudmouthed, mad-game Macy. He drove his knees forward. But as he neared half court, he began to slow. His air was gone. His legs were heavy. It felt like running through molasses. And the blister burned like fire.

"No, Martin!" Coach Clayton was in his ear again. *What did this guy have for lunch*? Cody wondered. *That breath could gag a maggot!*

"Martin, I don't care if you lose your breakfast along with your lunch! Don't you quit! Don't you quit on me!"

Cody pumped his arms fiercely. He caught Brett ten feet from the end line. They finished in a dead heat. Emphasis on *dead*. Cody pressed his body against the wrestling mat. It felt cool against his face. He tried to stay upright, but his legs failed him. He crumpled to his knees, then flopped onto his back. He felt his heart jackhammering in his chest. The ceiling lights overpowered his eyes. He closed them. *Just leave me here*, he thought. *Don't make me move 'til morning.*

Cody wondered how much time had passed when he felt someone kicking the sole of his right shoe, kicking him right in the blister. He opened his eyes and stared up at Pork Chop, standing at his feet.

Chop extended a thick right arm. "Come on, Cody. You need to walk it off before you stiffen up like a dead carp."

Cody felt himself being pulled to his feet. He marveled at Pork Chop's strength.

"Thanks, Chop."

"Ain't no thang. Let's get out of here before Coach makes us run the bleachers or something."

Cody followed Pork Chop toward the locker room. At the doorway, he felt a hand on his shoulder and turned to face Coach Clayton. "You did it, Martin! You didn't let him score. You saved the game, Martin! You see, that's why we run like this. So we can be ready. And we *will* be ready."

Cody nodded.

"And you, Porter, way to hustle! You move well for a big man. You remind me of Charles Barkley. You know Barkley, don't you?"

"Sure, Coach," Pork Chop answered. "We get ESPN Classic. I know all the old-timers."

Coach Clayton's eyes widened. "Old-timers?"

Pork Chop cocked his head. "Yeah. It's not like he plays anymore. He's from back in the nineties. You know—old school."

Cody felt the warm water cascade over him, washing away the sweat of a first hard workout. Some of his fatigue seemed to wash away, too.

Four more days of tryouts. First cuts would be announced tomorrow. He thought about his chances. Coach Clayton would probably keep twelve guys. Cody had been tenth or eleventh man last year, but Hooper, who was the last seventh grader cut, was back this year, and he had some game. He had gone to two summer camps and had turned himself into a fundamentally sound player, even if he was only an average athlete.

And Terrance Dylan, the new guy from Michigan, was tall and tough. He had crazy hops, too. He would probably crack the starting five.

Matt Slaven, last year's twelfth man, had grown a couple of inches. He was at least five foot eight—two inches taller than Cody. He still couldn't shoot to save his life. He was strictly a shot-blocker and rebounder. But he was a threat.

"Good practice, Martin," Pork Chop called as he entered the large square communal shower area.

"Thanks. You too. I think you'll start again this year."

"Could be. But you—you must have impressed Coach tonight. He wouldn't pay so much attention to you if he didn't think you were worth it. And you've got pretty good speed. You're even faster than I am now. I think you'll move up in the rotation. Maybe even to sixth or seventh man."

Cody stepped gingerly from the shower, wrapping a threadbare white towel around his waist. "I don't know. I think I'm on the bubble. Everybody's bigger, better, and faster. I guess we'll see. I gotta bounce, Chop. See you tomorrow."

"Yeah."

As he left the locker room two minutes later, Cody heard Pork Chop, still in the shower, doing a rap version of "Thank God I'm a Country Boy," at full volume.

At first the cold night air had felt refreshing after the sticky heat of practice. But now the air felt—well, cold. Cody wondered if his dad had forgotten to pick him up—again. He headed back into the school. There was a pay phone in the lobby. He tried the door. Locked.

"Hey—hold that door!" said a voice calling from behind him. The voice came from Gabe White—or maybe it was Wyche—a stocky, square-headed guy Cody had seen around town. Cody didn't think he was in high school anymore but wasn't sure whether he had graduated or just dropped out.

"I can't hold the door for you. It's locked."

White-Wyche approached Cody and glared down at him. "Are you mouthing off to me?"

"No, not at all. It's just that the door is locked."

"I can see that, pinhead! But it wouldn't be locked if you hadn't let it close behind you, would it?"

"No, you don't understand. I didn't let it close. It just—uh—"

Cody felt himself being pushed backward. His head hit the door with a deep thump.

White-Wyche spoke slowly through gritted teeth. Cody could smell beer on his breath. "I need to get in there. But I'm freezin' out here—all because of you."

A few silent seconds passed, then, "You got any money?"

Cody slid his hand into his hip pocket and produced the $20 bill Dad had given him. *Why am I handing this over?* he asked himself. *Probably to keep from being beaten to a bloody pulp.*

"This will do," White-Wyche said, snagging the money from Cody's hand. "This is your penalty." He grabbed Cody by the collar of his coat and spun him away from the door. "But maybe I'll toss you in the snow and stomp a mudhole in you anyway, just for laughs."

Cody heard the door open. He hoped it would be Coach Clayton. It was only Pork Chop. *Only Pork Chop*, he wondered to himself. *I didn't think I'd ever put those three words in the same thought.*

"So here's a question," Pork Chop said evenly, sizing up Cody's attacker. "Are you able to turn loose of my friend, or do you need some help?"

White-Wyche sneered. He had four inches and probably twenty pounds on Pork Chop—and at least five years.

"Let's go, Fat Boy. I don't mind butchering two punks for the price of one."

He shoved Cody backward. Cody tumbled into the snow. He looked around nervously. *Well, at least it's not the snow I puked on.*

Cody watched as Pork Chop and his larger aggressor squared off. He tried to think of an appropriate biblically based response. What would Elijah do? Probably call down fire from heaven. But that option wasn't open to twenty-first-century teens. What would Samson do? Find a donkey's jawbone and go upside White-Wyche's block head with it? Fine, but Cody Martin was no Samson. Besides, there was never a good jawbone around when you needed it. What would Jesus do? Good question. In this case, too good of a question. But even Jesus prayed.

Please, Cody prayed as Pork Chop staggered back from a hard roundhouse punch to his head, *help us!*

Tattoo Angel

In Sunday school, Cody and his friends often debated about what angels look like. Did they wear the traditional white robes, have elegantly styled hair, and large wings? Or were they ghost-like, shape-shifting entities without distinct features?

No one had ever guessed that an angel might weigh 220 pounds, have a shaved head, wear a black hoodie and ripped blue jeans—and sport a tattoo of a rattlesnake on his right forearm. But that was precisely the type of angel that had pulled White-Wyche off Pork Chop Porter and dug a vicious uppercut into his stomach.

White-Wyche dropped to his knees, as if he had suddenly found religion at Grant Middle School and decided to pray on the spot.

"You okay, Chop?" Doug Porter asked his brother.

"I'm fine, DP. I think I could have taken him. He was gettin' tired."

"How many times did he hit you? Because I'm going to hit him at least that many times. Only harder."

"You better think twice," White-Wyche gasped. "You don't know who I am. I got friends."

"Yeah?" Doug said, yanking his opponent to his feet. "I *do* know who you are. You're Gabe Weitz. You're just another dropout. And you don't have that many friends. *I'm* the guy with friends. Twenty-one of them. They're called the starting varsity football team. Offense and defense. And a lot of them are pretty big, just like me. So you get your friends, and we'll meet you anytime, anyplace." Doug turned to his brother. "How did this all start anyway, Chop?"

"He jumped my friend. You know Cody, don't you? He played wide receiver for us."

"Yeah, of course, I know Cody Martin. I'm sorry about your mom, dawg." Doug paused for a moment. "Hey, you catch any passes this season?"

Cody stood and brushed snow from his pants. "Yes, sir. Six. Two for touchdowns."

"Outstanding, Martin! Hey, did this guy hurt you? Want me to hit him a coupla times for you, too?"

"No. That's okay. But I *would* like my money back."

Doug formed an "O" with his mouth and turned on Weitz. "You stole money from a kid?"

No answer.

"Okay. I want you to give my friend here all his money back. And all y*our* money, too. And you can either give it up, or I'll knock you out right now and take it from you."

Weitz reached into his pocket and removed a small wad of bills.

"I don't want his money—just mine," said Cody, taking back his twenty, then handing the balance to Doug. "I'm not a thief."

Doug started to pocket the money and then paused. "You know, Martin, I'm not a thief, either. But still, this guy should be fined."

With that, Doug squeezed the money tightly and then tossed it onto the roof.

"Hey, that's my money!" Weitz protested.

"Not anymore, genius," Doug said, drawing his face within inches of Weitz's. "But if you want it, I can throw you up there so you can fetch it. Or you can let it go and determine in your heart and mind that you won't get in the face of my little brother or his friend ever again. This way, you'll just lose some cash, not your blood, many of your teeth, and perhaps a few of your vital organs. You're a lucky man. It's too cold for me to truly enjoy beating you down. But if you ever touch my brother or his friend again, I'll bring the pain. Got that?"

Weitz looked up from his stomach, which he was holding with both hands. "That fat kid is your brother? But he's—"

"That's right, moron. He's black—mostly, anyway. My brother is a brutha! You got a problem with that? And by the way, he's not fat—he's just big-boned. Give him one more year, and he'll beat you like a piñata on Cinco de Mayo. Now, you wanna say anything else about my brother?"

Still holding his stomach, Weitz shook his head and hurried away.

"And you let me know if you and your girlfriends ever want to dance with the varsity, you hear?" Doug called after him.

Then the defending state-champion heavyweight wrestler and all-state fullback turned to Cody and Pork Chop. "So who's hungry for tacos?"

When Doug's Camry pulled into the driveway, Cody could tell his house was empty. Only one light was on. When Dad was home, the place was lit up like an appliance showroom. Cody had noticed that since his mom died, Dad had seemed to develop some sort of weird fear of—or at least distaste for—the dark.

"The old man's not home, eh, Cody?" Pork Chop observed. "That's weird that he forgot to pick you up."

"He probably just had to work late. Again. Thanks for the ride, guys. And thanks for keeping that guy from whupping my tail."

"T'aint no thang," Doug laughed. "I needed to scrap. I was gettin' rusty. I was gonna bring the war down on him. But that guy had no game. Woulda been no challenge."

Cody shook his head. "He had no brains, either. He had to be as dumb as a box of rocks! Who in his right mind woulda thrown down with you? And, uh, Chop, I want you to know that I was going to jump in and help you—before Doug came. I was just kinda stunned for a minute."

"It's cool, Cody. I know you had my back. But I was doing okay. I'd love to run into that guy in another year. I'll be as big as you, Doug, so you better watch out."

Doug flexed his right bicep. "If you ever even dreamed of getting guns like this, you'd wake up and apologize."

Pork Chop, apparently stuck for a response, belched loudly.

Cody opened the car's back door. "I'll let you guys sort this out on your own. Thanks again for the ride."

He walked carefully to the front porch, making his way by the meager light that spilled from the living room window. He fished the key from under the welcome mat and let himself in.

Sinking heavily onto the living room couch, he wondered where Dad was. There was probably an explanation-apology on the answering machine, but he didn't feel like listening. The excuses were growing old.

He retrieved the TV remote from the coffee table and began scrolling through seventy-six cable channels' worth of entertainment options. As he made his way through the fifties, Cody slowly shook his head. Nothing but infomercials, old game shows, and shop-at-home programs. Next came a documentary about, as best as Cody could tell, cactus, then a "shocking, behind-the-scenes story" about an actress he had never heard of.

At least there was ESPN, now only two channels away. You could always count on ESPN. He hit the channel-advance button twice and set the remote down.

"Welcome to the National Aerobics Championships," proclaimed an overly perky woman.

"Welcome to my worst nightmare come true," Cody muttered as he clicked off the TV and went upstairs.

Slowly, he entered his parents' room and flicked on the light. The closet was closed, and Cody knew he shouldn't look, but the temptation was too strong. He took a deep breath and slid the mirrored door open.

They were still there. Mom's clothes ruled three-fourths of the closet space: dresses in bright colors, a few sweat suits—mostly off-brand stuff—and a modest collection of T-shirts from 5K and 10K races. She had tried to keep running, even after the cancer had claimed much of her energy. But gradually, her running gave way to slow walks with his dad, and finally rides in a wheelchair, but only on days that weren't too cold.

Her shoes, neatly paired, occupied exactly one-half of the floor. Dad's work boots and decrepit canvas high-tops looked lonely and shabby on the other side.

Cody shook his head sadly. Women from the church had offered to sort through Mom's clothes and donate them to worthy charities, but his dad always put them off. In the months following the funeral, his polite-but-firm response was always, "I'm just not ready to deal with that right now."

Cody wondered if his dad would ever be ready. Since the death of his junior high sweetheart three months ago, his dad's work hours at the paper had escalated. When he was home, he sat in his black overstuffed recliner, staring blankly at the television set, which was usually tuned to CNN.

However, in recent weeks, Cody had discovered Dad watching—or to be more accurate, not watching—the wildlife channel, the cooking channel, and even the home-repair channel. This would have made Mom laugh, because when anything in the house malfunctioned, Dad's first move was to the "Repair" section of the Yellow Pages, not his meagerly supplied toolkit.

Only two nights ago, Cody had awakened at 2:12 a.m. and slipped downstairs to find Dad asleep and snoring like a tractor while Deputy Dawg rounded up a band of law-breaking Siamese cats.

As he stood there looking at his mom's clothes, Cody thought of how she used to watch Saturday-morning cartoons with him when he was a kid—and how she actually seemed to enjoy them.

That's when it happened again, like a kung fu kick to the heart. She was gone. She would never wear those clothes again. She'd never do that rat-a-tat-tat laugh while watching TV with him. She wouldn't be sticking report cards to the fridge with her magnets that looked like fruit. He was on his own when it came to figuring out the well-hidden meaning of contemporary poetry. The taste of her homemade chocolate chip cookies was only a memory now.

Perhaps worst of all, she would never again run down the bleachers to congratulate him after a win or console him after a loss. What were you supposed to do when you lost your number-one fan?

He put his back against the wall and slid to the floor. Heaving sobs overtook him—the kind that always left his eyes red, his abs aching, and his head throbbing.

He wasn't sure how long he had been on the floor, curled up like a crying newborn, when he heard the front door creak open and then close softly. He scrambled to his feet and rushed into the master bathroom. Behind the locked door, he fought to bring the crying under control. He tried to think of something positive, like basketball. But he couldn't think of that without thinking of her. It was hard to think of anything without thinking of her.

He heard a light tapping at the door. "Cody, you okay in there?"

Cody sniffed. "Yeah."

"You sure? Do I hear you crying?"

"Sorry. I'll try to cry softer next time."

Tense, silent seconds passed. Cody knew that later he would have to ask forgiveness, from his father and his heavenly Father.

"Hey, lose the attitude." Dad's voice was coming to a slow boil. "My life is hard enough, okay? Let's cut each other some slack."

Cody opened the door. "I'm sorry, Dad. I shouldn't have said that. I don't know where it came from." He dabbed at his eyes with a washcloth.

"It's okay, Cody. Let's dry up the waterworks now. Crying isn't going to bring her back."

"I know."

"Let's both hit the sack. I'm beat. We can talk at breakfast if you want."

"Sure," Cody replied. They hadn't eaten breakfast together in at least a month. Most days, he heard Dad's Geo pulling out of the driveway just as he was waking up for school. And on the weekends, if Dad didn't go into the office, he slept until noon—sometimes later.

Just before sleep conquered Cody's weary body, his dad peeked his head into his room. "Hey," he whispered, "I forgot to ask how tryouts went. You gonna make the team?"

"Yeah," Cody said, praying that it wasn't a lie.

"Great! I'll come to more of your games this season. I promise. I know I made it to only a few last year."

"Just one, actually, if you're talking about basketball."

"Really?"

"Really."

"Well, we'll have to do better this time around."

"Yeah. We will."

Chapter 3

Cuts That Don't Heal

Day two of tryouts was shaping up to be, in Pork Chop's words, "chocolaty good." After a half hour of drills, Coach Clayton divided up the twenty-five basketball hopefuls into five teams for full-court scrimmages.

The scrimmage rules were simple. Five minutes on the clock. Only those defensive actions that drew blood or left a bruise were considered fouls. When the five minutes were up, the winning team stayed on the court. The losers sat.

Coach placed Cody on a team with Alston, Pork Chop, Bart Evans, and a sharp-boned point guard named Bradley Lang. Cody's team took the court first and won six games in a row. Alston was shooting lights-out, Pork Chop was a beast under the boards, and Cody clamped on each opposing small forward like a bear trap. Brett Evans hit two fall-away jumpers over him in the first game. No one scored on him after that. Cody even got a congratulatory chest bump from Alston when he blocked a Matt Slaven baseline jumper, smacking it off the exit sign at the gym's north end.

"Looks like we have a juggernaut here," Coach Clayton observed after Pork Chop tipped in a missed shot to seal victory number six. "We're going to have to make this more interesting. I'm getting bored. Gannon, your team's up next, right?"

"Right, Coach," the freckle-faced point guard said.

"Okay then. We're gonna make a little trade, just like they do in the NBA. Martin, you join Gannon's team. And Hooper, you run with Alston's unit. Oh, and one more thing. Martin, you guard Alston. Should be a nice change of pace. Nobody's guarded him all night."

Cody sighed. "But, Coach—"

"Is there a problem, Martin? Was anything I just said unclear to you? Because I—can—speak—more—s-s-s-s-slowly—if you need me to."

"No, Coach, it's just that I'm a forward, and Alston's a—"

"A guard! That's right, Martin! He's a guard, and that's want I want you to do. Guard a guard."

Alston walked by Cody, slamming the ball into his gut and driving the wind from him. Cody felt tears rising in his eyes.

"Just call me your bus driver, Martin," Alston whispered, "because I'm gonna take you to school."

Cody waited for an effective comeback to form in his brain. Nothing developed. He felt as if his mind were a blackboard that someone had erased—and then thrown away the chalk. He shrugged his shoulders and inbounded the ball to Gannon.

Gannon dashed down the floor. Before Cody had even crossed midcourt, Gannon stopped at the top of the key and launched a high-arcing, nineteen-foot jumper. The problem was that the top of the key was twenty feet from the hoop.

Good old Greg Gannon the Cannon, Cody laughed to himself. *Never saw a shot he wouldn't take.*

Pork Chop collected the air ball and fired an outlet pass to Alston, who dribbled straight for the top of the other key. Cody smiled. He knew Alston—that he was going to take the same shot Gannon had just missed. Show him who the team's true sharpshooter really was! Alston's aim was better than Gannon's, but not much. His shot clanged off the front of the rim and was going to drop into Cody's waiting hands.

No need to even jump for this one, Cody thought. *It's coming right to me.*

He extended his arms and waited for the ball's arrival. Just before the leather touched his fingertips, Alston came around Cody's right shoulder like a blur. He leaped into the air, giving Cody a close-up view of his hairy armpit, snagged the ball, and, before his feet touched the ground again, banked it in off the glass.

Alston retrieved the ball as it dropped neatly through the net and then planted it on the end line.

"Nice rebound, Martin," he said. "Way to sky for that ball!"

With that, he laughed derisively and sprinted down court to play defense.

Meanwhile, Gannon was putting on a dribbling exhibition just past midcourt as Cody took his position on the left wing. Coach had threatened to throw Gannon "like a spear" if he took another bad shot, but Cody wasn't sure if the threat would be effective. He readied himself to charge in for a rebound just in case.

He never got the chance. Apparently not wanting to experience being a human projectile, Gannon passed the ball. And it was a beautiful pass. Gannon looked directly at Cody, then fired a no-look pass to Slaven on the high post.

Unfortunately, Gannon's no-look was so deceptive that Slaven didn't see it coming. Slaven's proud nose took the full impact of the pass, and blood began to trickle from both nostrils.

Cody looked at Coach Clayton. Would he whistle the action to a stop? After all, blood had been spilled. Then again, no one had committed a foul. Inattention like Slaven's wasn't wise, but it wasn't illegal.

While Cody was thinking, Alston was hustling again. He grabbed the ball, which was rolling away from Slaven's feet, and launched into a one-man fast break.

Cody responded quickly. He sprinted after Alston, drawing alongside him as he veered in for a right-handed layup.

Time for retribution, he thought. *A well-timed leap, an emphatic block, and maybe Cody Martin will be the bus driver for a while.*

Alston pushed hard off his left foot and leaped toward the hoop. Cody jumped with so much force that he heard himself grunt, just like Pork Chop when he threw the shot put.

Alston put good arc on the ball, and at the apex of his jump, Cody knew he couldn't block it. However, he was sure that Alston had shot his layup too hard and too high. It was a bad shot, almost as if Alston had done it on purpose.

Reality hit Cody too late. Alston had already moved to the left side of the hoop, where he collected the ball as it came off the glass. He squared his feet and hit an easy two-foot jumper.

Angry at himself for being suckered, Cody forgot to
get his landing gear down properly. He landed awk-
wardly on his left ankle, stumbled, and crashed into
the back wall. The wrestling mat kept him from
cracking his head, but he felt a hot needle of pain
shoot into his ankle. He tried to take a step on it and
felt it start to buckle. Carefully, he sat on the floor to
assess the damage.

He saw Alston standing over him, holding the basketball. *Is Alston going to offer to help me up?* he
wondered. *Or at least ask if I'm okay?*

Alston shook his head in mock sadness. "Nice
defense, your gracefulness. Martin, you are so getting
clowned. Right in front of Coach, God, and everybody. I only wish your girlfriend was here to see this."

"I don't have a girlfriend," Cody snapped, too loudly.
All heads turned in his direction.

"Right. That Robyn chick with the funky glasses?
The one who's a better player than you are? You love
her, and you know it."

"She's just my friend," Cody protested.

"Not if she could see the way you're playing. I bet
you get cut tonight."

"Alston!" Coach Clayton's voice was weary but
firm. "That's enough."

"And Martin, go see Dutch and get some ice on the
ankle. Goddard, you come in for Martin. And please,

for the love of Bill Russell, won't you try to play a little defense on Mister Alston before he starts thinking he's All-World?"

Coach Clayton paused and studied his clipboard. "Oh, and one more thing. Glazer, Turner, and Martin, I want to see each of you in my office after practice tonight."

Cody shot a glance at Coach Clayton and then looked away. He felt as if something huge—Doug Porter, for example—had just crash-landed on his chest.

Cody limped the length of the locker room, pausing occasionally outside Coach's closed office door to strain his ears for bits of the conversation with Turner. But it was all murmurs and mutters. Glazer had left ten minutes ago, the veins in his moist eyes looking like tiny red branches. He had offered Cody a quick, wounded glance, and then bowed his head and trudged away.

Moments after that, Pork Chop had come in. Chop was uncharacteristically quiet. He lightly slapped Cody on the back, as if he were trying to kill a mosquito. Then as he turned to leave, he said, "Call me, Cody. Tonight. No matter what happens."

Cody sat down in front of his locker. He looked at his ankle, trying to determine if it looked swollen. He rose to pace again, then forced himself to sit. Coach had ordered him to "stay off that bad wheel," but anxiety kept driving him to his feet.

He looked at his watch. Turner had been in there for eleven minutes now. What were they talking about? Would Turner exit crying too?

I should probably say something to Turner, Cody thought. *I should have said something to Glaze.* He tried to think of a Psalm or Proverb about comfort, but nothing came to mind.

Cut. That's what he was going to be. He bounced the word around in his head. Cut, cut, cut, cut. Cut! He remembered sixth grade, when he had sliced a blueberry bagel and his left hand along with it. Mom had bandaged that cut and dozens of others through the years. But now she was gone. And besides, there was no Band-Aid that could help a cut like the one Coach Clayton was about to give him.

Chapter 4

Smells Like Team Spirit

You look like you're gonna eject from that chair, Martin," Coach Clayton observed. "Sit back. This is gonna take a while."

Cody tried to relax on the cold metal folding chair that faced Coach Clayton's desk. The coach sat on his desk, rather than behind it, his long, narrow feet dangling only an inch from the floor. He cleared his throat. "Martin, do you know why you're here?"

Cody thought of the two tearful departures he had witnessed within the past half hour. He stared at Coach Clayton's game-weary Converses.

"No, Coach. Not really. I'm—I'm sorry about what happened at the tail end of practice. I don't know what was wrong with me. I was just having a bad day. I—uh—think I was getting tired near the end, and—"

"Tired, Martin? I don't think so. You're probably the fittest guy out there."

No excuses, no excuses, no excuses, Cody told himself. He felt tears forming and tried to blink them back. *What doesn't kill you makes you stronger. What doesn't kill you makes you stronger.*

He had recited that line a hundred times during Mom's funeral. It kept him from crying then. Maybe it would work now, too. He felt Coach's eyes on him and forced himself to move his eye contact from shoes to face.

"Martin, do you know what the hardest thing is for a basketball coach to find these days?"

Cody shrugged.

"It's defense, my man. Big D." Coach Clayton hopped from his desk and began to pace the length of the office, which took him six strides, round-trip. "Defense is hard and dirty work, Martin. And in this age of showtime, run-and-gun basketball, few athletes have the will to play hard-nosed, all-hustle, in-your-face-like-an-insurance-salesman d-e-e-e-e-fense!"

Cody swallowed hard. *Here it comes. The gripe session for letting Alston school me.*

"Martin, you're not the fastest guy on the team, are you?"

"No, sir."

"And you're not much of a leaper. And even though I'm impressed you can shoot with either hand, your shot needs some work."

Great, great. Let's give a detailed list of all my flaws. What's next? My haircut's ugly, and I have six zits on my face?

Coach Clayton stopped pacing and stood in front of Cody. "But there's one thing you can do, Martin. And that—never mind what happened tonight against Alston—is play me some defense."

What game is this guy playing? Okay, I got your point. I'm no good at anything but defense, and tonight, with making the team on the line, I didn't even do that. Just cut me already, so I can call my dad and tell him I'm a failure. That's just what he needs right now. No wife and a loser son.

"Do you know what I'm trying to say to you here, Martin?"

"Um, that I'm good at only one part of basketball, and when I'm up against somebody talented, I'm not even good at that?"

Coach Clayton leaned forward and smacked his hands together so loudly that Cody almost ejected from his chair.

"No! Cody Martin, I have you in PE. I watched you play football this year. I talked to Coach Murphy about how you guys stacked up in hoops last year. And during these tryouts, I've watched you like Pork Chop watches dessert being served at Mamie's House o' Pies. Here's the juice, my man. You can cover anyone in this league—Alston, Rick Macy, Keenan Jones, anybody."

Coach Clayton settled himself on his desk again. "But you cannot get all nervous or starstruck, or whatever you were out there tonight. I didn't know if you were gonna guard Alston or ask him for his autograph."

"I'm sorry, Coach."

"You *should* be sorry, Martin. Good grief! Is Jason Kidd on our team?"

Cody thought this could be a trick question, but he coaxed the obvious answer from his mouth.

"No, sir."

"Correct! Is Michael Jordan making another comeback and using our league to tune up?"

Cody managed a small smile. "No."

"You'd better believe it's 'No'! Those guys don't play here. Neither do Larry Bird or Magic Johnson. Neither does Pistol Pete, may God rest his soul. So you see, all I'm asking you to do is guard thirteen- and fourteen-year-old boys. Boys pretty much like you—only a few of them, like Alston, have facial hair. But that doesn't make them players. If that were the case, Santa Claus would be MVP in the NBA. You got that, Martin?"

Cody nodded.

"Listen, son, this league has enough pretty boys, showboaters, and posers, But we're woefully short on dawgs."

Cody cocked his head. "Dogs?"

"Not 'dogs,' Martin! Dawgs! D–A–W–G–S. This team needs a pack of wild, defense-crazy dawgs, and I want you to lead 'em!"

"Me, Coach?"

"Yes, you, Numb Noggin'! I want you to play that gnarly, in-your-face D I've seen you play, save for about two minutes earlier tonight. I want you to lead the league in floor burns. And I want more than that. I want you to swat shots like a horse swats horseflies, which you can do with those long monkey arms of yours. Man, for the love of Kevin McHale, you have some long arms on you! Use 'em! Also, I want you to steal like Jesse James. I want to put you on every team's best scorer—and I want you to drive him crazy. I want you to be all over him like a nasty, burning rash that just gets worse and worse the more he scratches it!"

Coach Clayton hopped from his desk again. "Stand up, Martin."

Cody stood slowly and found himself staring into Coach Clayton's Adam's apple. The scene reminded him of Rocky Balboa and Ivan Drago in *Rocky IV*. "You feel how close I am to you, Martin? You experiencing the ambiance of the pastrami sandwich I wolfed down right after practice? It's uncomfortable, isn't it?"

Cody nodded.

"That's how I want you to make every opponent feel." He palmed a basketball from his desk and bounced it slowly, punctuating each name. "Macy. Washington. Jones. Locke. Cabrera. And, when we practice, that's how I want you to make Alston feel. He needs that. He needs the work."

Coach Clayton handed the ball to Cody. "This is your ball now, Martin. It's a game ball. And from now on, I want you to think that every ball is yours. When the other team has it, they're just borrowing it, understand? You gotta think, 'That's my ball, and I'm getting it back.' I don't care if you steal it, rebound it, or have it left to you in a will—you get that rock back. You put the bite on every glory-grabbin' gunner in this league, okay? I want you to be my dawg. Are you my dawg, Martin?"

Cody smiled, "Yes, Coach."

Cody watched Wednesday tryouts from the bench. Dutch, the team's stocky trainer, shuttled him fresh ice packs on the half hour—for his head, not his ankle. His ankle was only mildly sore, but he had awakened with a fever he figured was over 100 degrees. His dad wouldn't have let him go to school, but he was gone when Cody woke up.

Before practice, Coach Clayton felt his forehead and tried to send him home, but Cody protested, saying, "I want to stay and be a watch-DAWG!"

The coach chuckled. "Watch-dawg! I like that. Okay, Martin. You can stay. Just don't breathe on anyone."

Coach Clayton ran the team through agility drills, then set up mini-scrimmages again. He put Gannon and Alston on the same team, and they alternated launching shots from twenty feet and beyond. Combined, they hit about one-fourth of their attempts.

While Gannon and Alston dueled for the title "King of Deep Downtown," Pork Chop's team dominated. Chop planted himself in the low post and powered in an assortment of hook shots, turnaround jumpers, and drop-step lay-ins. Anyone daring enough to get in his way ended up being body checked out of the play—and sometimes on the seat of his pants.

On Thursday, Coach Clayton held Cody out of scrimmages, "just as a precaution," but he was allowed to shoot free throws and go through passing drills. When it was time to scrimmage, the coach hand-picked what Cody was sure would be the starting five for the season opener—Brett Evans and Dylan at forwards, Pork Chop at center, Alston and Lang at guard. This quintet abused all comers.

From the bench, Cody watched Alston like a cop on a stakeout. He noted that Alston drove to his right eight out of ten times, loved to use the behind-the-back dribble to elude a defender on a fast break, and, when double-teamed, tended to leap into the air first, look for options second.

Next time I guard you, Cody thought, *I'll be ready*.

That night Coach Clayton went cut-crazy again. He dismissed everyone but Gannon, Pork Chop, Alston, the Evans twins, Dylan, Slaven, Sam Hooper, Lang, Mark Goddard, and Cody "Dawg" Martin.

At the beginning of that Friday's workout, Coach Clayton gathered his eleven players at midcourt.

"Congratulations, Raiders," he began. "You're the team. I'm keeping only eleven guys this year, because that's how many are good enough to play ball for me and not embarrass themselves, their country, their school, or their immediate and extended families. You see, in my system, everybody plays. I don't believe in carrying benchwarmers. If I want my bench warm, I'll set it on fire."

In the two weeks leading up to the season-opening invitational "Grant Hoops Classic" tournament, Coach Clayton focused on creating game-like situations. He drilled the basics of the 2–1–2 zone defense and the half-court trap. He installed an offense in which nearly everything went through Pork Chop on the high post. And he devised a never-fail way to beat a man-to-man full-court press—"Give the ball to Alston, and everybody clear out of his way!"

And everyone shot free throws—lots of them. Twenty at the beginning of practice, ten in the middle, and fifteen at the end.

"You need to get used to shooting under various levels of fatigue," the coach told his team after a particularly grueling practice session. "You must shoot the ball the same way, whether you're fresh as a daisy or dead-dog tired. I'll be here every morning at 6:30 a.m. if anybody wants to come in and improve this part of his game."

Cody showed up the next morning. Bart Evans was the only other Raider in the gym. Coach Clayton shot them both a quick smile.

"Good to see you, men. Try to get a hundred makes. Keep track of how many shots it takes to get you there. And a month from now, I think you'll see a big difference."

At practice that night, the team scrimmaged under game conditions. Coach Clayton pulled Cody aside and instructed him, "Dawg Mister Alston everywhere he goes."

"I'm gonna dissect you, Martin!" Alston whispered, as he crossed midcourt on the opening possession.

Cody said nothing. Then he pretended to go for Alston's unconvincing fake pass to Slaven on the right wing. And when Alston fired a bounce pass toward Dylan on the left wing, Cody pounced on it like a cat on a mouse.

As he drove in for an uncontested layup, Cody heard Coach Clayton whoop and shout, "Nice D, Martin! Great anticipation!"

This was followed by, "Alston, if you're going to telegraph your passes, why don't you just save yourself the trouble and broadcast them over the sound system? I can fire up the announcer's mike if you want."

The next time Alston brought the ball upcourt, he faked the pass to his left, then went right, just as

Cody suspected he would. The pass was crisper this time, so Cody didn't get a clean steal. But he did bat the ball downcourt, where Gannon scooped it up and charged to the top of the key, his favorite location from which to miss a shot.

Gannon's line drive smacked hard off the backboard, and everyone froze, expecting Coach Clayton to blow his whistle and launch into his Gannon-tailored lecture on shot selection. When the coach did neither, Gannon chased down his miss, drove to the basket, and carefully laid the ball into the hoop.

Alston swore and tried to catch Cody napping, pushing the ball up the right side of the court. Cody picked him up before he reached midcourt. On cue, Alston dribbled behind his back, trying to move the ball from his right hand to his left. Cody darted to Alston's left side and poked the ball away before he could regain control. Five seconds later, he laid the ball into the basket, left-handed. He hoped Coach Clayton noticed that he went lefty.

Late in the scrimmage, Alston hit two rainbow jumpers with Cody right in his face. But Cody's team, made up of mostly second teamers, won the scrimmage 20–18.

At the end of practice, Coach Clayton assembled the squad on the front row of bleachers.

"Raiders," he said, "you're lookin' tough. We have a legitimate shot at taking the tournament, even with Central and Mister Rick Macy in the field. But we're at opposite ends of the bracket, so we'll have to make it to the finals to discover if Macy's all he's cracked up to be."

"Coach, can I say something?" The question came from Alston, who usually said nothing, unless he was trash-talking.

"Sure, Mister Alston. What's on your mind?"

"If Martin D's up on Macy the way he did me tonight, we can beat Central—get revenge for the three times they spanked us last year."

Pork Chop nudged Cody with his elbow and whispered, "Did you hear that, Cody? Alston big-upped you! Will wonders never cease?"

Cody shrugged. "Apparently not."

On a cold Friday afternoon in November, Grant faced Maranatha Christian School in the opening round of the tournament. It was, as Coach Clayton noted after the game, "the worst mismatch since Michael Jackson married Lisa-Marie Presley." The final score was 40–18, Raiders.

Cody and the second unit entered the game late in the first quarter and hit the Lions with a full-court press that made crossing midcourt seem like crossing the Red Sea—without the waters being parted.

In the second round, on Saturday morning, Grant dismantled Holmes. Apparently the Holmes coach didn't scout the Raiders in the first round, because Cody and his Dawg Pack forced thirteen first-half turnovers, resulting in ten easy baskets.

As he did in the Maranatha game, Coach Clayton called off the Dawgs when the lead reached twenty points. Final score: 42–24.

To no one's surprise, Grant squared off against Central for the tourney championship on Saturday afternoon. During his pregame pep talk, Coach Clayton grew so excited that he kept breaking chalk sticks as he tried to diagram plays and defensive adjustments on the locker room chalkboard. He had to finish drawing up an inbounds play with a stub of chalk no bigger than Cody's little toe.

"Gentlemen," he said, brushing chalk dust from his just-bought blue jeans, "on paper, Central has a stronger team. But thank heavens, this game is played on hardwood, not paper. I have a feeling that if we can keep the score close, we might get an opportunity to steal the game at the end."

Cody didn't know his coach's religious affiliation, but on this afternoon he would prove to be a major prophet.

Chapter 5
Laying It on the Line

Near the end of a fiercely competitive championship battle, Cody watched the leather sphere teeter on the edge of the front rim.

"Come to me, ball," he whispered.

As if on command, the ball dripped off the iron. Cody blasted off from the hardwood like a 120-pound rocket. To his left, he saw Macy rising with him. That could be trouble. Macy was five foot nine, three inches taller. And he had decent hops.

Cody willed his body to go higher. He stretched his arms and extended his fingers. The ball settled onto his fingertips.

As soon as Cody touched down, he made eye contact with the referee under the basket. He knew there had to be less than five seconds on the clock. The Raiders needed a time-out. He was about to make a "T" with his hands when Macy landed—right on top of him. Cody's head erupted in sparks of pain.

Cody blinked and watched the world slowly come into focus. He realized he was lying in the middle of the free throw lane, looking up into Coach Clayton's red, watery eyes.

"You okay, Cody? I think you were knocked colder than my ex-mother-in-law's heart."

Cody touched the top of his head gingerly. He winced as he felt an egg-size lump. He tried to arrange his words before he spoke.

"I think I'm okay, Coach. My head hurts, but I'm all right, I guess. Hey—did I draw the foul?"

The corners of Coach Clayton's mouth curved upward. "Yes, you drew the foul."

"All right! So, I make two free throws, and it's game over?"

"That's how it works, Cody. Two from the charity stripe, and we're Grant Hoops Classic champs. Are you okay to shoot?"

"Yeah, I guess so. But, Coach?"

"Yes?"

"It's true what they say about seeing stars."

Coach Clayton smiled again. "Right now I just need you to see yourself hitting two from the line."

Coach Clayton extended his hand and pulled Cody to his feet. The partisan crowd clapped enthusiastically. Macy came over and leaned his head close to Cody's. To the packed Grant Middle School gym, it looked like a show of sportsmanship.

"I think your rock head cracked my elbow, Martin." Macy sneered.

Cody tried to muster a confident laugh. "I think it's the other way around."

"Sure hope the pain doesn't affect your concentration—or your aim. It would be a shame to choke in front of your home crowd and cost your team the championship. Think about that when you toe the line."

Cody thought of several responses, none of which would please Blake or his dad, who were sitting behind the Raider bench. So he settled for a blank stare.

Macy gave Cody a fraternal pat on the back and took his place along the perimeter of the free throw lane.

Cody stood at the line. The scoreboard read Grant—47, Guest—48. Only three seconds remained on the clock.

"Okay, gentlemen," the squatty referee said. "We're not in the bonus, so it's one and one. Play the miss."

"That's right," Cody heard Macy hiss. "The miss-s-s-s!"

Cody felt his knees turning to oatmeal. The ball felt heavy and foreign in his hands.

This stinks! he thought. *Is this ball regulation size? It feels too big. I don't even know if I can get it to the rim. Aw, that's all I need—to lose the championship on an air ball!*

He wondered what Coach would say—what his teammates would say. He thought of how everyone would look at him in the hallways on Monday—how they would whisper behind his back and wag their heads disappointedly.

Why does it have to be me? God, what have I done to deserve this? Why can't Alston be up here? He lives for this kinda stuff. Maybe I could faint right now. If I can pull off a convincing face-plant, maybe Alston can shoot for me. I think there's a rule that provides for a sub—

The referee's whistle snapped Cody from his thoughts. He pried the ball from Cody's tense fingers. "Time-out, white," he called.

Cody shook his head. Calling a time-out to ice the shooter was good strategy, but not your own shooter. He and all the other puzzled Raiders circled around Coach Clayton on the sideline.

"What's up, Coach?" Alston asked. "Why did you call a time-out at a time like this? Martin looks like he's about ready to cry."

"Terry," Coach Clayton began, "shut up—please. Let's remember who the coach is."

Alston dipped his head and muttered something Cody couldn't decipher.

"I have good reason for this TO. To celebrate the championship, we're all going to Louie's Pizza after the game."

He pulled his cell phone from the breast pocket of his well-worn, navy-blue blazer. He punched in a number and held the phone to his right ear. "Mike," he yelled, as the Grant Middle School band began its assault on 'Sweet Georgia Brown,' "Coach C. here. Listen—those victory pizzas we talked about earlier today? Start making 'em. We'll be there in about twenty-five minutes. Yeah, that's right. Pitchers of pop, too. And hang on a minute, Mike—"

Coach Clayton looked at Gannon. "Gannon, you're still a vegetarian, right?"

Gannon nodded his head sadly. "Yes, my mom's still forcing me."

Coach Clayton yelled into the phone again. "Yeah, I'm still here, Mike. Listen—make one of those pizzas all veggie, okay? Gannon and I are vegetarians, at least for this weekend."

The coach said goodbye and slipped his phone back into his pocket. He scanned the eyes of his team. "Any questions?"

No one said a word. Even Alston could only manage a weak whistle.

"Okay then. You'll all need to hustle and get showered after Cody drains these two shots. I want to get to Louie's while the pizzas are still hot. And your parents are invited, by the way."

The Raiders broke their huddle and headed back to the game. Coach Clayton tugged on Cody's jersey.

"Cody, it's six-thirty, you got it? It's six-thirty."

Cody started to frown, but then a small smile of recognition creased his face.

He walked to the line, closed his eyes, and took a deep breath. *It is six-thirty*, he assured himself. *It's early in the morning, and I'm here, as I am every weekday. Won't leave the gym until I hit a hundred free throws. One hundred. These are just two more. It's just me, a ball, and a hoop. No crowd. No distractions.*

He opened his eyes. He dribbled the ball three times, then brought it to eye level, his fingertips finding a seam. He made sure his right elbow was straight and close to his body. Now the ball didn't seem large and foreign. It felt perfect as it rested on his fingertips, as if it belonged there. He eyed the rim, bent his knees, and flicked his wrist.

He knew when the ball left his hand that it would find nothing but net. The crowd exploded into cheers and roars of approval, but the noise seemed faraway. Cody wanted the rock back—now.

Macy was saying something to him but it was lost amid the noise.

The ref handed him the ball. "One shot, gentlemen. Play the miss."

"There isn't going to be any miss," Cody whispered. He went through the routine again. Dribble, dribble, dribble. Ball to eye level. Elbow straight. Bend the knees. Release, rotation—

The ball splashed through the net. Gannon and the Evans brothers raced to congratulate Cody, but he was already sprinting downcourt. He knew that neither team had a time-out left, so the Grizzlies' only hope was a long pass and a miracle catch-and-shoot.

On the inbounds play, Clay, the Grizzlies point guard, lobbed a desperation pass that went right to Pork Chop at midcourt.

Interception! Cody thought, as the nasal blare of the buzzer signaled the end of the game.

Cody had been in a few midcourt victory celebrations, but never as the center of attention. He felt a hoard of hands patting his shoulders and back. He wondered if one of them was Robyn's. His eyes met Coach Clayton's. The coach raised his arms and pointed to his watch. Cody saw him mouth the word "pizza." He began to swim his way through the sea of bodies to the locker room.

It was only three blocks to Louie's, so Cody had told his dad he would walk to the party. He stood at center court of the dark gymnasium, his basketball under his right arm. He released the ball and dribbled four times, listening to the dull echo of leather on hardwood. He looked to the rafters.

Father God, thank you for today, he prayed silently. *You know how Dad and I feel about praying over winning or losing a basketball game. You have my word that I'll never do that. I'll just keep praying to represent you. So I didn't ask you to help me make those free throws. I think you have more important things to worry about. But somehow I felt you were with me there on the line. And I thank you for that. I think the only thing that kept me from fainting was knowing that you love me no matter what. And by the way, thanks for this game. I really love it. I want to play it 'til I die. And then—well—I hope there's basketball in heaven. Amen.*

Cody pushed a wet comma of cinnamon-colored hair up on his forehead and dribbled slowly toward the free throw line, the same place he had stood thirty minutes earlier. He hit twelve free throws before one curled out. Then he made two more.

You know, God, the coolest thing about today wasn't that I helped us win a championship. It was how happy it made everybody. Thank you for that. Especially for making Dad happy. He needs that.

Cody heard street shoes clicking on the court. It was Blake. "Your dad's saving us seats at Louie's. I thought you might be here."

Cody fired a chest pass, which Blake caught adroitly. "Yeah. I'm sorry, B. I just don't want to leave the court. It's like there's magic here."

Blake thumped his right fist against his chest. "I think the magic is in here, you know? Cody, you really represented your school well this afternoon."

"Thanks. And thanks for coming to the game. It means a lot to me. Hey, B?"

"Yeah?"

"My mom—do you think she could see me today?"

Blake smiled sadly. "You always ask the toughest theological questions, Cody."

"Well—"

"I don't know, man. Here's what I think—and this is just my opinion. They didn't teach me this at Biola. I believe that heaven is a place of perfect happiness. I believe your mom can see all she needs to see to be perfectly happy. So if your game is part of that equation, I think she saw you. And if not, maybe she can read about it in 'The Heavenly Gazette' or something. Or maybe an angel can give her a report, like on ESPN."

"Yeah. Maybe. You know, she used to watch ESPN with me. She was the only mom I know who did that."

Cody saw that Blake's eyes were moist. "I'm sorry," the young pastor said quietly. "I'm sorry about the loss you and your dad are feeling. Mind if I give you a hug?"

Cody mustered his best brave laugh. "Dude, you have been to too many of those men's retreats. I'm okay, really. But thanks. Maybe you can hug Pork Chop when we get to Louie's. He'd *love* that."

"I'm not risking getting between Porter and his pizza. Speaking of which—"

"Okay, I hear ya. Let's go eat. But hey, B—guess what? Macy stuck his pumpkin-sized head in the doorway before he got on the bus tonight. He yelled, 'Hey, Martin, you were lucky on those free throws— I'll see you later in the season, then again at Districts! In *my* gym.'"

"What did you say?"

"Nothing. I just turned around and hit a jumper from the baseline. But he *will* see me at Districts— 'cuz I'm gonna be right in his face. I hope Mom can see that one, because I am going to put on a show! And I'm going to shut Macy down. He got only ten on me tonight. Next time I'm going to do all I can to hold him to single digits. I doubt that anybody's ever done that."

Cody held the door for Blake as they left the gym. Then, before he let the door swing closed, he turned to survey the quiet court. "I don't know if you could see it or not, Mom," he whispered. "But that one was for you."

Chapter 6
Gut-Bucket Greta

On Monday morning Cody walked down the science hall and noticed the masses parting in front of him, like the Red Sea during the Exodus. For a moment he hoped this was in response to the previous Saturday's game-winning heroics, but then reality grabbed him by the collar and shook him to his senses. He knew that Greta must be walking behind him.

It had started in the beginning of seventh grade, when Greta enrolled at Grant. On her first day, Alston and a few of his stooges noted her pimple-littered face, Salvation Army-reject clothes, limp, greasy hair, and distinctive aroma—a pungent combination of cheap cigar smoke and body odor. They quickly dubbed her

"Gut-Bucket Greta," after the containers that fisher-
men discarded the entrails in after cleaning fish.

At first this moniker was used behind Greta's back,
but then it became more public. "Gut-Bucket Greta
at three o'clock!" or "Greta alert!" someone would
shout, whenever she came down a school hallway or
entered the lunchroom. Then some of the students
would hold their noses until she passed by.

Andy Neale, Alston's best friend, had taken the
ridicule to an even lower level during Greta's second
month at Grant. While trying to avoid brushing
shoulders with her in the English hall, he had lunged
against the wall, holding his nose and faking the dry
heaves. Alston had doubled over with laughter, and
soon he and several other students did their own
variations of the Neale wall hug whenever Greta
approached. They gagged, they pressed their bodies
against lockers, and they shouted personal hygiene
tips such as "Why don't you take a bath, you pig?"

By mid-seventh grade, the students' tormenting of
Greta was less vocal but no less regular. As if it were
their sacred duty, ninety-nine percent of the student
body consistently treated Greta as if she were a leper.

Cody never participated. He caught flack for it for
a while. During layup drills, Alston would yell "Gre-
ta-a-a-a-a-a!" whenever Cody short-armed a shot.

Neale razzed Cody, too, but only when Alston was around. At times, Cody felt proud of himself for refusing to join in the taunting. He wondered how he could tell Blake about the stand he was taking, because he was sure Blake would be proud of him. He hoped he could work it smoothly into a conversation, so it wouldn't seem like boasting.

On the other hand, Cody made sure he was never caught walking directly beside Greta. He would quicken his pace to pass her in the hallway, or curl off toward a drinking fountain if he saw her coming toward him.

Robyn Hart was a different story. She did much more than shoot eye-daggers at Alston and his entourage. Any time she and Greta traveled the Grant hallways at the same time, she drew right next to her, sometimes linking her hand through the crook in Greta's elbow, like a rock star's security guard. And she rotated her head, like a tank turret, daring anyone to hurl an insult or launch into a fit of sound effects.

A few times, Cody noticed her whispering into Greta's ear as they walked the gauntlet together. Greta never showed much emotion. She tucked her chin to her chest and took quick, light steps toward wherever she was going. She didn't even seem to acknowledge Robyn's presence.

During the week leading up to Grant's regular-season basketball opener, Robyn took her Greta support to a new level. Outside the gym's north doors, she stood in the middle of the lobby and delivered what came to be known as the Sermon in the Foyer, brandishing her vocabulary like a sword.

"You bunch of gutless me-too monkeys!" Robyn began, addressing the approximately thirty students plastered against either side of the walls. "*You* are the ones who make *me* wanna puke! What has Greta Hopkins ever done to any of you? How do you think she feels about coming to this school every day? Think for one minute how you would feel. You are making every day hell for her. You are hurting her. You have hurt her over and over and over again. She endured this all last year—all year! Think about that! And now you're doing it again this year! It's time for you to stop!"

Cody approached the scene midway through Robyn's sermon. He heard the word "stop" echoing in the hall and saw Robyn with her arm around Greta's shoulder.

For a moment, Robyn was silent, but Cody knew she wasn't done. She was only reloading. While Robyn prepared her next volley, the futuristic "wop" of the tardy bell filled the air, and the congregation began to stir.

"Nobody leaves!" Robyn ordered. To Cody's surprise, almost everyone stayed, perhaps more out of shock than obedience. "You have damaged this girl enough. It stops today. It's time to start acting like human beings. You can start by telling Greta that you're sorry."

That brought a snort from Neale. Robyn whipped her head around to face him. "You have a problem with being a human being, Andrew Neale?"

Neale looked to Cody. "Hey, Martin—control your woman, would ya?"

Cody tried to will a witty yet heroic response from his mouth. He needn't have bothered.

Robyn marched toward Neale, stopping when her nose nearly touched his chin. "Why don't you control me, Andrew? You think I'm afraid of you, just because you're one of Alston's tools? That doesn't impress me."

Neale took a step backward. "Who cares what impresses you, wench?" he said.

Cody felt Robyn's eyes on him. This was his cue to beat Neale like a kettledrum. But he felt the strength seeping from him, like the air from an inner tube with a slow leak. He sized Neale up. They were about the same size and build. Neale was pale as a mime; the only sports he played were the computer variety. His jaw was definitely his strongest muscle. But still—

Cody took a tentative step toward his potential opponent. Who was he supposed to be in a case like this, long-suffering brother Joseph, or jawbone-wielding Philistine slayer Samson? "Hey—" he began.

Neale spun around to face him, their eyes locking on each other like tractor beams.

This wouldn't be such a bad time for the second coming, Cody thought. He waited a moment to hear a trumpet blast or some rolling thunder.

Instead, he heard a booming voice, but it wasn't the voice of the Lord. It was that of Principal Prentiss, and it was impressive in its own right.

"Did we not hear the bell, people?" he asked.

At that, the students scattered like ants. In the frenzy, Cody lost sight of Neale. He followed Robyn into the life science classroom and took his customary seat behind her. After she sat down, she twisted around in her chair. "So, Cody—were you going to defend my honor out there?"

Cody shrugged.

Robyn frowned.

Cody balled his right hand into a fist and smacked it into his left palm as hard as he could. Robyn smiled at him and then turned around as Mrs. Emmons began her scintillating lecture on the frog's digestive system.

The open Greta abuse didn't vanish completely in the days following, but roughly half of the former antagonists decided to become neutral. Alston and his gang still went through the motions, probably as much to test Robyn as to insult Greta. Robyn didn't deliver any more speeches, but she made sure to cling to the wall, plug her nose, and hold her breath—puffing out her cheeks as if she were storing plums in them—each time Alston, Neale, or any of the Alston posse passed her in the hall.

Cody's heart hammered whenever this happened. *One of these days*, he thought, *one of those guys is gonna say something really vile to Robyn, maybe even slap her or something. And then I'm gonna have to "defend her honor," even though I don't truly know what that means.*

Cody hoped that if someone retaliated against Robyn, it would be Neale or one of the weak members of Alston's mangy pack. He prayed that it wouldn't be Alston himself. Alston would turn his face into hamburger.

Meanwhile, the Raiders opened regular-season play—and made hamburger of their opponents.

In the season opener at Holy Family, Cody didn't start, but Coach Clayton put him into the game two minutes into the first quarter, after Keenan Jones schooled Brett Evans on three straight possessions.

"Martin!" Coach Clayton barked. "Next to me—now!"

Cody left his position at the end of the bench and stood eagerly in front of his coach.

"Sit!" Coach Clayton said.

Cody obeyed.

The coach coiled his arm around Cody's shoulder. "You're still my dawg, right, Martin?"

Cody smiled and nodded.

"Okay then. Get out there and take a bite outta Keenan Jones. He's killin' us."

Cody approached the scorer's table and pointed to the number 15 on his jersey. When the ref waved him into the game, he pointed at Brett, who shook his head and trotted toward the bench.

"Good luck, Cody," Brett said as he passed by. "KJ's even faster than last year. Watch that jab-step of his."

Cody nodded and picked up Jones on the right wing. Not surprisingly, Mack—Holy Family's point guard—fed the ball to the team's star immediately. Jones shot Cody a quick smile, jab-stepped with his left foot, then drove right, toward the baseline.

Cody moved with him like a shadow. He got to the baseline a half second before Jones and planted his foot on it.

You're gonna have to go out of bounds or plow right over me if you want to get to the bucket this way, Cody thought.

Frustrated, Jones picked up his dribble. He tried to head fake Cody into the air, but Cody stayed on his feet. He had seen that head fake work on Brett. Jones pivoted away from Cody, looking for help.

Unfortunately, his teammates had cleared the entire right side of the floor, expecting their captain to dominate any one-on-one matchup the Raiders threw at him. Jones had no one to pass to. Cody could see the panic in his eyes.

The referee blew a rippling blast on his whistle. "Five-second violation," he called. "Red ball!"

On Holy Family's next possession, Young—a pear-shaped five-foot-ten center—came out to the right wing to set a pick on Cody.

"Pick left!" he heard Pork Chop shout.

Cody nodded. As he felt Young close in, he deftly stepped around the pick and cut off Jones as he drove to the basket. Again, Jones stopped his dribble, held the ball above his head, and scanned the court for help.

As Jones's eyes darted left and then right, Cody saw him relax his grip on the ball.

Like a boxer throwing a jab, Cody shot out his left hand and poked the ball free. Alston picked up the loose ball and dashed upcourt. Cody followed, about three strides behind.

"You got help behind you, T!" he shouted.

Alston angled for the middle of the lane. Mack, who had hustled back on defense, appeared to be in position to thwart Alston's drive. Alston rose toward the basket, holding the ball high over his head with his left hand, like a waiter delivering a pizza. Mack leaped to defend the shot—and appeared to be high enough to block it.

But Alston didn't shoot the ball. With a flick of his wrist, he passed it over his left shoulder, into Cody's waiting hands. With Alston screening Mack, Cody had a candy five-footer, which he banked off the backboard for the score.

As Cody headed back to play defense, Alston drew alongside him. He said only one word—"Sweet!"

Cody did his best to keep his smile from spreading all the way across his face.

For the duration of the game, Jones never released a shot without struggling to get it over, around, or under Cody's active hands.

Jones finished the game with eight points, four on free throws. Grant won, 43–29. Cody looked at the scoreboard as the final buzzer sounded and recalled that last year, Jones had scored twenty-nine on the Raiders—all by himself.

Grant faced East in the second regular-season game. Cody started, for the first time in his basketball life. Coach Clayton assigned him to Bobby Cabrera, who, next to Macy, was the best shooting guard in the league.

Coach Clayton's pregame instructions to Cody were simple. "Dawg, you stick to Cabrera like stink on a skunk!"

Cody complied. He cut off passing lanes, overplayed to Cabrera's dominant left hand, and countered every drive with quick footwork.

With three minutes to play in the first half, Cabrera had yet to score. Frustrated, as Cody mirrored his every move during a full-court press, Cabrera launched an elbow at Cody's throat. Like all of his shots, this attempt missed—sort of.

Cabrera's bony elbow glanced off Cody's left shoulder. He took two steps backward and looked to the lead official for a foul call. The lead man had missed the elbow, but the ref trailing the action saw it all.

He whistled a technical foul, then clamped his right hand on the back of Cabrera's narrow neck and marched him to the East bench, where his coach stood, wagging his head in disapproval.

Cody felt Pork Chop's hand on his shoulder. "You okay, Cody?" Chop's face was red with anger.

"I'm good, Chop. That one might leave a mark, though. But you know how the chicks dig bruises." He forced a laugh.

Pork Chop didn't appear amused. "Hear me now, Cody. Cabrera will pay. I'm gonna foul him so hard that his family is gonna cry out in pain—and that includes the relatives who are already dead!"

"It's okay, man. Don't retaliate. We're spanking 'em. That's what counts. Bruises heal, but a loss stays a loss forever."

Pork Chop nodded unconvincingly.

East's coach kept Cabrera out of the game until late in the third quarter. Then, as he jogged onto the court, he detoured in Cody's direction.

"Stay off me, Martin," he said evenly, "and keep those long monkey arms down. Or I'll stick you again."

"I'm just playing the game," Cody said quietly. He hoped he could count on that proverb about a gentle answer turning away wrath.

The third quarter ended without incident. Grant held to a ten-point lead as the fourth quarter began. On East's first possession, Cabrera took a pass on the left wing and blasted toward the basket. Cody anticipated the drive and moved into position to roadblock Cabrera's move. He braced for the impact that he knew would come. Just before he collided with Cody, Cabrera dipped his shoulder and caught him squarely in the stomach.

Cody felt the air being forced from his body. He hit the floor with a groan and a thud.

Well, maybe I didn't turn away all *his wrath*, Cody thought as he struggled to breathe.

Both refs tagged Cabrera for charging, but that didn't appease Coach Clayton. He sprung from the bench.

"That was a flagrant foul!" he shouted. "For the love of Dennis Rodman, get that punk outta there!"

As both refs went to calm Coach Clayton, Cody saw Cabrera standing over him, like a victorious gladiator, his arms crossed in front of his chest.

"You got something to say, Martin?" The question was bait, and Cody knew it.

"Just two words," he half-gasped.

"Yeah? Let's hear 'em."

Cody rose to his feet and looked Cabrera in the eye. "Our ball," he said.

Thirty seconds later, Pork Chop issued his own statement. As Cabrera chased Alston through the lane, Pork Chop left his man and set a vicious pick. Cabrera didn't see it coming, and the impact was like a poodle colliding with a refrigerator. Cody wasn't sure if the cry that rose from Cabrera's lungs was in pain, shock, or both. He slumped to the floor as if someone had removed all his bones.

Pork Chop smiled and raised his right hand high over his head, acknowledging a foul.

After the game, which Grant won 48–36, Pork Chop and Cody stayed late and took turns shooting free throws.

"Did you see that pick, Cody?" Pork Chop said with a laugh. "If Cabrera has any fillings, they're loose now!"

Cody smiled sadly. "You didn't have to do that for me, Chop. I told you that."

Pork Chop left a free throw an inch short. "Well, maybe I didn't do it for you. Maybe I did it just for me."

Cody rolled his eyes. "My turn to shoot."

As he positioned himself at the line, Cody saw Robyn enter the gym's south doors, sipping a can of root beer. She angled straight for Pork Chop, who was standing under the basket.

"Good game, Deke. The way you played makes me hungry for girls' season to start. And that was cool how you stood up for Cody out there."

Pork Chop gave her his best aw-shucks shrug. "Ain't no thang."

Robyn was smiling, but Cody didn't like the look of her smile. "No, it *was* a 'thang,' Deke," she said. "It's noble to defend someone. Very noble."

Pork Chop went into full shrugging mode again.

"Too bad you don't defend someone who really needs it—in real life, not just in a game."

Pork Chop froze in mid shrug. "'Scuse me?"

"I can't excuse you, Mister Porter. Not as long as you do that up-against-the-wall garbage like Alston and his mindless followers. And don't you deny it. I've seen you."

Pork Chop looked to Cody for help. Now it was Cody's turn to shrug.

"You at a loss for words, Deke Porter?" Robyn said, snapping off each word like a bite of licorice rope. "That's a first."

Cody had rarely seen Pork Chop this helpless, at least outside of algebra class. He thought of the Weitz incident and the approximately nine-hundred other times Pork Chop had saved him from severe beatings. He cleared his throat.

"C'mon, Hart," Cody said. "Chop's not like those other guys. He's not vicious or anything. He's just being a goof, you know? Hey—he even teases me sometimes."

Pork Chop nodded enthusiastically. "Yeah, I'm always bustin' on Cody about his bird legs and spaghetti arms. I goof on everybody." He paused and eyed Cody, who was nodding encouragingly. "Besides," Pork Chop said slowly, "if Greta would take a bath and wash her clothes once in a while, she wouldn't catch so much abuse."

Cody saw the color rise in Robyn's face. "Can you hear yourself, Deke Porter? Can you hear what's coming out of your mouth? Do you think Greta is at fault for her problems? Do you think anybody would choose to be the way she is?"

"I dunno. I mean . . . maybe she doesn't know any better. She does seem kinda slow."

Robyn ripped the ball from Cody's hands and fired a baseball-style fastball at Pork Chop's knees. Chop tried to leap and avoid being hit, but, as Coach Clayton often pointed out, the Raider post man "couldn't jump over the Manhattan phone book— Manhattan, Kansas!"

The ball struck Chop's right kneecap with a smack and ricocheted almost fifteen feet.

"What's wrong, Deke?" Robyn said, her voice dripping sarcasm. "You seemed 'kinda slow.'"

Pork Chop was doubled over, rubbing his knee as if it were a magic lamp. "That was harsh, Robyn. Can't a brother get some love? I can't believe you did that. On my bad knee and everything."

Robyn snorted. "You don't have a bad knee."

"I do now."

"If all you have is a bad knee, you're way ahead of Greta, Deke. She has a bad life. And you're responsible. You can't deny it. And then you have the nerve to suggest she's slow! Ugh!"

Cody went to retrieve the ball, which had eventually rolled to midcourt. He stooped to pick it up and then paused. He stood and, with his left foot, booted it softly to the other end of the court. Best not to give Robyn another shot at Chop.

He walked slowly back to the conversation, or inquisition, or whatever it was.

Robyn was invading Chop's personal space in a big way. She kept stepping toward him, and he kept retreating. Eventually his back was plastered to the gym's south wall, and for all of his 190 pounds of farm-built muscle, he looked as helpless as a newborn kitten.

"Let me ask you this," Robyn said, continuing her interrogation. "You say Greta is mentally deficient—how do you know? Have you ever talked with her—and I mean besides hurling hateful insults at her?"

"Well, no. But *nobody* talks with her."

"Wrong, muscle head. I talk with her. She's a smart girl. She's poor, but she's sharp."

Pork Chop shook his head slowly. "I just don't understand. If she's smart, then, why, uh—"

"I'll show you 'why-uh.' Come with me right now. Both of you."

Cody and Pork Chop flashed each other the same look. A combination of "What now?" and "Why me?"

"Robyn," Cody protested, pulling on his sweats, "where are we going? We're tired. We just won a big game—a tough game. We need some downtime. We just wanna go home and chill, you know?"

"No, I *don't* know. There's something more important than chilling, okay? There's something you need to see. Now. Deke, you have hurt an innocent girl. I want you to learn a little more about your victim."

She turned to Cody. "And you. You're not much better. You don't take part in the hatefests, but you don't do anything to stop them, either. Don't you remember what Blake said at that youth rally last summer? He's your youth pastor, for heaven's sake! He said, 'All that is necessary for evil to prosper is for good men to do nothing.' Do those words ring a bell up there in that head of yours? You are helping evil prosper. It's as simple as that."

Cody looked at Pork Chop, who raised his eyebrows and mouthed one word—"Busted."

With that, he jogged from the gym, as Robyn rained insults on him. "Go ahead—run away, Deke! You're too weak to face the truth, huh? You know, they shouldn't call you Pork Chop; they should call you Lamb Chop!"

That one caused Chop to stop, but only for a moment. Without turning around, he disappeared from sight.

"Keep up—will you, please?" Robyn called impatiently over her shoulder. "I'd like to get there before dark."

Cody quickened his pace, trying to keep up with Robyn's brisk steps without having to break into a jog. That would be uncool.

They had left downtown Grant—with its antique shops, shoe stores, donut shop, and Merv's Men's & Western Wear store—behind them. They were headed southeast, toward what Cody had heard people call "the wrong end of town." As they moved, Cody noted how patches of crabgrass and weeds pushed their way up through cracks in the sidewalk. They walked past a pawn shop, a rent-to-own furniture store, and three consecutive boarded-up storefronts, which used to house a dry cleaner, a pipe and tobacco shop, and the Log Cabin Chinese Restaurant, which Dad could never mention without rolling his eyes.

Once they were past the El Dorado Motel, whose weather-beaten sign proclaimed "NO ACANC," Cody and Robyn crossed the oil-stained asphalt of Chuck's Used Cars and veered due east toward Clear Creek. They followed the creek as it meandered out of town and into a land of high weeds and thick trees. The aspen leaves had already turned. The brilliant rusts, gold, and red were fading, and soon the winter winds would strip the trees bare until they looked like white skeletons.

Suddenly, Robyn held up her right hand, like a scout in an old western movie. "Be quiet now," she ordered.

"I haven't said a word since we left the school," Cody observed.

Robyn whipped her head around and narrowed her eyes at him.

Tentatively, he held up his fingers in a peace sign and gave her what he hoped was an endearing grin. She rolled her eyes, turned away, and resumed threading her way through a patch of tall wild grass. They crossed under Highway 7 and began a slow, steady descent. Cody had explored his share of Grant since moving there in second grade, but he was in unfamiliar territory now.

"Robyn—"

She turned to him and shushed him like a kindergarten teacher. "It's over there," she said quietly, "on the other side of the creek, about fifty yards north."

Cody leaned forward, squinting his eyes, because that's what those TV scouts seemed to do at times like this.

His eyes found it almost immediately—a battered yellow school bus, which looked as if it had been dropped from above into a clearing amid aspen trees and an assortment of mutant-sized weeds.

"What's that bus doing here?" Cody asked.

"Serving as Greta's home."

Cody studied the scene. "Is it even legal to live like that?"

"I don't know, idiot. But that's not really the point, is it?"

"Why is she living out here?"

"It's a long story. Greta won't tell me all of it. Let's just say it involves her mom's suicide, her dad's getting fired, and their house getting repossessed."

Cody started to speak, but he was cut off by a sudden burst of robust barking. A thick-necked, mud-brown dog charged into view, ears flat against its huge skull.

Is that a Rottweiler or a pit bull? Cody wondered. He felt his heart accelerate. Some dogs barked just for show, but he got the sense that this one meant business. Fortunately, the barking seemed directed at something on the other side of the creek, at a 45-degree angle from where he and Robyn crouched.

"Back off, Cujo!" called a voice in front of the dog.

Cujo complied in midbark.

"That's a good boy," Greta cooed, as she emerged from a cluster of aspens. Cody wondered if he had heard Greta speak before.

He turned to Robyn. "What's that in her hand?" he whispered.

"I'll give you a hint. In your house it's squeezably soft. But Greta's family can't afford squeezable or soft. Imagine life with no indoor plumbing, Cody. Imagine what it will be like for her when winter sets in and there's a foot of snow on the ground most of the time."

"I gotta tell Blake about this. Maybe our church can help them."

Robyn looked at Cody. She seemed on the brink of crying. "Cody?"

"Yeah?"

"A church can help, and that's fine. I know they will always be willing to do something. The question is, what are *you* gonna do? You know what the Bible says about helping the poor, the widows, the orphans, 'the least of these.' This is about as 'least' as it gets. You're seeing it with your own eyes. So forget the church for a minute—what are *you* going to do?"

"I don't know."

Cody saw disappointment in Robyn's eyes. "Well, then—you have some thinking to do, don't you? Maybe some praying, too."

The duo slipped away. They walked silently back to the middle school, where they parted ways. Before she left, Robyn gave Cody an earnest, pleading look that reminded him of his mom's face in those final weeks—when she needed a cushion adjusted, a painkiller, or just someone to hold her hand.

Cody sprinted upstairs to his room and read the parable of the Good Samaritan. *It's been too long since I read this one*, he thought. *Okay, God,* he whispered, as he smoothed the open pages of his Bible, *I get the message.*

The next Monday morning, instead of shooting free throws, Cody spent an hour talking with Coach Clayton. The subject of basketball never came up. On Tuesday morning Robyn and Cody arrived at the gym at 6:45. Greta was waiting for them. Robyn wrapped her arm around Greta's slumping shoulders and led her to the girls' locker room, where Coach Clayton and Miss Engle, the girls' basketball and volleyball coach, had arranged for her to shower every morning. Miss Engle also gave Greta a permanent locker, a privilege usually reserved exclusively for athletes.

In science class later that day, it was Cody's turn to put all the chairs on top of the tables so the cleaning crew could sweep and mop the floors. Typically, whoever had this duty left Greta's chair untouched. But on this day, as the students filed out of class,

Cody went to Greta's place first and placed her chair on the table.

As he moved from table to table, Cody felt someone watching him. He looked up and saw Greta, standing in the doorway. At the final table, he came to Andrew Neale's chair. He smiled at Greta as he tipped the chair onto its side and left it lying on the floor. As he left the room, she smiled back.

On Wednesday after lunch period, Cody saw Pork Chop, Neale, and a few others press their backs against the wall as Greta passed by. Cody approached Pork Chop and yanked firmly on his right arm. Pork Chop, looking puzzled, planted his feet and refused to be moved.

When Greta was out of sight, Pork Chop sighed and allowed Cody to tug him into the boy's bathroom.

"If you wanted me to go somewhere," Pork Chop said, "you coulda said 'please.'"

"I didn't feel like saying 'please' out there. But I do now. Chop, please—you gotta stop this Greta stuff. Check this out—the girl lives in an abandoned bus outside of town. No toilet. No running water. Her mom killed herself a while ago. They lost their house. And that's only the beginning."

Pork Chop shook his head sadly. "Man, that's rough. I had no idea. But, Cody, you gotta understand—I didn't mean anything vicious."

"It *does* mean something vicious to her. It hurts her. Every time Alston or one of his cohorts pulls something on her, it beats her down a little more. You may think you're different from them, but to Greta you're not. You're just another one of Alston's cruel tools."

Pork Chop took a step toward Cody. "Hey—I'm nobody's tool!"

Cody held his ground. "Then stop acting like one."

Pork Chop took a deep breath and then exhaled forcefully, just as he did when completing a bench press. "Okay, Cody. You're right. I'm sorry."

"Don't tell me. Tell *her*."

"Aw, I can't do that, dawg."

"Sure you can. I did."

"You did?"

Cody nodded. "Monday morning. I said it."

"What did she say?"

"Nothing. But she heard me, and she knows I meant it. That's what matters."

Pork Chop nodded. "Yeah," he said quietly. "You're right. I'm not promising I can bring myself to talk to her, but the harassing is done."

On Friday after first period, Cody saw a small crowd gathered in front of a row of lockers in the science hallway. Neale was leaning back against a locker, trying to look casual. Greta stood two feet in front of him, head bowed, arms crossed in front of her body.

Cody angled toward Neale, uttering a silent prayer as he walked. *God, please show me what to do here. And please let me keep all my teeth. Amen.*

As he drew up to Neale, three words flashed in Cody's head, like opening credits on a movie screen— LOVE ALWAYS PROTECTS. He smiled. "First Corinthians 13:7," he whispered to himself.

"What's up, Neale?" Cody asked, trying to sound confident.

"Nothing, Martin. I'm just kickin' back. But this ugly sow here seems to have a problem with that."

Cody turned toward Greta. "He's leaning against my locker," she said quietly. "I asked him to move. I asked him nicely."

Cody willed himself to look Neale in the eyes. "She asked you," he began, "and now *I'm* asking you. C'mon, dude—move. We're all gonna be late for class."

Neale snorted. "You want me moved? You move me. And I don't see your fat slob, half-breed body-guard around. You're on your own."

"So are you. Alston's not here to have your back either. Now, move. Or I *will* move you."

Cody studied Neale. His arms hung loosely at his sides, but he looked as if he could go into fighting mode instantly. His expression was hard to read.

Neale looked as if he were trying to solve a complex algebra equation in his head.

Seconds crawled by. Cody could feel his armpits growing moist. He was glad he remembered to use his deodorant that morning.

Love always protects. Love always protects. But how was he supposed to protect Greta—and not get expelled or beaten to a pulp?

Cody raised his right hand slowly and scratched his ear. Then, quick as a rattlesnake strike, he lashed out at Neale, smacking the locker with his palm. He missed Neale's head, just as he had planned—but only by inches.

Neale leaped from Greta's locker, as if it had suddenly delivered an electric shock to his backside. He also squealed like a piglet.

That drew a roar of a laughter from the onlookers. Crimson-faced, Neale began to back away from Cody.

"I'm out for now," he said, "but this isn't over, Martin. You best watch your back, Cuz." Neale's voice sounded threatening, but he continued to back up as he spoke.

"You don't have to watch your back, Neale," Cody said evenly. "Because if I see you harassing her again, I'll come for you—and it'll be straight on."

Cody turned his attention to Greta. She loosened her small, rigid mouth and gave him her second smile of the week. Cody grinned in return. The morning showers and makeup tips from Robyn hadn't transformed Greta into a stunning beauty. After all, this was Grant Middle School, not a production of *Cinderella*. Greta was still a plain-looking girl. Clean, but plain. Still, she had a nice smile.

After the Cody-Neale showdown, almost everyone in school quit going into wall-hug mode in Greta's presence. But not Terry Alston.

The following week, Cody arrived in the science hall after first period. The scene was identical to the one a few days earlier, except this time it was Terry Alston camped in front of Greta's locker, like a watchdog. Neale, Schutte, and a few other of Alston's sycophants stood nearby, taunting Greta in their nasal voices.

Cody walked grimly toward Alston. He knew that getting pummeled by Alston and his homeboys wouldn't get him a place in the next *Jesus Freaks* book, but he hoped that Blake would use a "Cody the Courageous" story the next time he preached for Pastor Taylor—or maybe at *his* memorial service.

Cody whipped around as he felt a strong hand on his shoulder. He hoped it was a teacher. It was Pork Chop, looking uncharacteristically grim and shaking his head slowly from side to side.

"Hey, Chop," he said quietly. "Don't try to stop me. I gotta do this. Just come and visit me in the hospital. Or say a few kind words at my funeral."

Pork Chop's head was still moving. "No, Cody. I got this one."

Cody couldn't stop the sigh of relief before it escaped from his throat. "You don't have to—"

"Cody," Pork Chop interrupted, "I've been thinking about what you said, okay? And you were right. And then what you did last week—that showed me something. I guess you could say you inspired me. Now, like I said, I got this. You just watch my back in case one of Alston's monkey boys tries to jump on it."

Cody nodded solemnly.

"Yo, T," Pork Chop called as he and Cody reached Greta. "Step off from Greta's locker, or I'll put you through it."

Alston's hands were at his sides, but Cody saw them curl into tight fists. "Try it, fat boy. I can hit you ten times for every time you tag me."

Pork Chop shrugged. "One time is all I need. And don't call me fat. I prefer the term 'big-boned African-American.'"

The ripple of Coach Clayton's whistle preempted Alston's response. The coach loped toward the scene, with smooth, ground-gobbling strides. Cody felt a twinge of disappointment. The "Fight of the Year" had just been postponed.

"Problem here, fellas?"

Alston spoke up first. "Nah, Coach—we were just talking."

"Yeah?" Coach Clayton's voice was laced with suspicion. "Well, you best save your breath for the extra suicides you're all going to run tonight. My athletes get to class promptly, understand? They don't hang out and clog up the hallways. Now, all of you—get to class!"

As the students dispersed, Cody heard Alston address Pork Chop in a conspiratorial whisper, "Someday, Porter, you and I are gonna war!"

Pork Chop smiled good-naturedly. "I know," he said. "Meanwhile, I'll just keep stacking hay, pumping iron, and sparring with Doug in our basement, waiting for that fateful day to come. I'm gettin' thicker and stronger every day. What're *you* gettin'?"

Grant faced a disorganized Cook team and a tired Lincoln squad that week, beating both by twelve—on the road. In the Lincoln game, Cody held Locke, a five-foot-nine power forward who was averaging fourteen points a game, scoreless. At halftime Locke was zero for eight, and Coach Clayton issued a challenge to Cody,

"Martin, if you blank Locke in the second half, I'm buyin' hot-fudge sundaes for everyone after the game."

Later, when Cody tipped just enough of Locke's last-second turnaround jumper to make it fall short, the entire Grant bench ejected from their seats, whooping and clapping.

"That's my white boy!" Dylan screamed.

"No, that's *my* white boy," Pork Chop countered.

Coach Clayton smiled. "That's my dawg!" he said.

Locke ended the game zero for fourteen. After the final buzzer, he rebounded his errant shot and punted the ball into the rafters.

Week four of the hoop season brought Maranatha and Mill Creek to the Grant gym. The Raiders won both games but lost something more important. In the fourth quarter of the Mill Creek game, with Grant leading by two, Alston tried to block a Mike Riley fallaway jumper from behind. He was whistled for a foul and immediately drew nose to nose with the referee. About the only three clean words Cody heard from Alston during the thirty-second tirade that followed were "you," "blind," and "moron."

The ref responded by assessing Alston his second technical foul and ejecting him from the game. Alston marched from the court, snatched a towel from Dutch, and sat heavily at the end of the bench.

Coach Clayton followed Alston down the bench, kneeling in front of him and whispering something in his ear. From his vantage point at midcourt, Cody could see Alston's eyes widen and his head shake in disbelief. Coach Clayton drew to his feet and stood over his star guard, hands on hips. Alston rose slowly and slinked away to the locker room.

After Riley hit his three free throws, Coach Clayton called time out. "Men," he said, his voice measured, "we're going to have to win this one without Terry Alston. Losing your cool is like spilling a box of Cheerios. It's messy, and it takes a lon-n-n-n-g time to get your stuff together afterwards."

Cody nodded. Blake had talked about the same thing on Sunday—only without the cereal analogy. His words had come straight out of Proverbs 16:32— "Better a patient man than a warrior, a man who controls his temper than one who takes a city."

Cody had never thought of himself as being stronger than Alston, but maybe, in at least one important way, he was.

Before the Raiders broke their huddle, Coach Clayton looked almost pleadingly at his team.

"This is the last game before Christmas break," he said, "so we'll have a long time to think about it if we lose. C'mon fellas—we can win this thing if we play tough D. That's defense, Gannon. That thing we do while you're waiting to get the ball back."

Gannon grinned, winked at Coach Clayton, and jogged to midcourt.

"Heaven help us," Coach Clayton sighed.

As he took up position on the left wing, Cody looked up at the game clock, which read 1:31. Gannon charged up the middle of the court, and Cody and Pork Chop shot each other a foreboding glance as they moved in to rebound the inevitable Gannon miss.

I wonder if this will be a clanker off the front rim or an air ball, Cody thought as he battled Riley for position in front of the hoop.

Gannon was just inside the top of the key when he launched his jumper. Riley tried to hip-check Cody aside as the ball flatlined toward the bucket. Cody held his ground, went into a slight crouch, and prepared to jump for the rebound.

Cody relaxed his leg muscles as Gannon's shot whipped through the net. He saw Gannon do the Tiger Woods fist-pump as he jogged back on defense. However, as he crossed the center stripe, Gannon jump-stopped and pivoted back toward the Raider basket. Riley had just released a lazy inbounds pass to Brach, his backcourt mate, and Gannon got to the ball well before it reached its intended target.

Gannon collected his prize and elevated for a jumper from the right wing. Cody fought his way down the center of the lane for the rebound. Out of the corner of his left eye, he saw Gannon release his shot at a severe downward angle.

In the split second that followed, Cody realized he was witnessing a triple miracle. First, Gannon had actually made a shot. Then, he played defense. And now, with the game on the line, he was declining a cherished opportunity to shoot, in favor of a potential assist.

Cody caught the bullet jump pass in stride and hit a left-handed layup. As he hustled back on defense, he saw Coach Clayton jumping up and down, his heels nearly hitting his backside.

"He looks like a cheerleader," Cody whispered.

"An ugly cheerleader," Pork Chop agreed.

Energized by Greg Gannon's rare display of complete basketball, Grant pulled away to win by seven. The Raiders entered the Christmas break 9–0.

Chapter 7
Un-Merry Christmas

Cody's dad turned down no fewer than five invitations to Christmas dinner, including one from his sister in Oregon. Dad also had a brother in Texas, but he rarely spoke of him—or *to* him—as far as Cody knew.

On December 22 Cody heard a knock at his bedroom door. He put down his Bible and called, "Yeah?"

Without opening the door, his dad asked, "Cody what would you like to do for Christmas? It's coming up so fast, and I really don't know what to do."

Cody rose from his bed and opened the door.

"I don't care what we do, Dad. I just don't want you to go to any trouble. Around two, Blake will pick us up to volunteer at the soup kitchen, just like always. Then Pork Chop is coming by a little later. Other than that—"

"I just can't do the soup kitchen thing this year, Cody. There's no way."

Cody looked closely at his dad. His face bore deep lines, as if they'd been etched with a sculptor's tool. Had they been there for a while, or was this something that sadness did to a man?

"Really, Dad?" he said. "I mean—Mercy House has been kinda like a family tradition."

"Well, we're not quite the same family this year, are we?"

Cody felt anger rising inside him. He fought to push it down.

"Okay, Dad. I'll do Mercy House on my own. As for the rest of the day, I guess I'm not sure. What do *you* want to do?"

"I don't really feel like celebrating, to tell you the truth, Son, but we could go spend part of the day with one of the church families. We have plenty of invitations. It's just that . . . without your mom, I'm just not looking forward to Christmas this year."

Images flashed through Cody's head like movie clips. Mom reading Christmas letters from friends and relatives. Mom sticking holiday photos on the refrigerator with those fruit magnets of hers. Mom lining the fireplace mantel with greeting cards. Mom smiling as she welcomed guests into their home and humming "Silent Night" as she put away leftovers.

He heard Dad clear his throat and snapped from his memory trance.

"Well," his father said in a weary voice, "should we go somewhere or what?"

"Nah, Dad. Let's just have a quiet Christmas, you and I. We don't have to eat turkey or any of that stuff. We can just eat . . . whatever. And if you want, you can shoot hoops with me and Chop when he comes over."

His dad smiled sadly. "Your mom adored Deke Porter. It will be nice to see him. And maybe he can help us eat all those gift baskets. There are at least ten on the kitchen table, and it's still not Christmas yet. We could start our own fruit stand."

Cody forced a laugh. "Hey, Dad?"

"Yeah?"

"On Christmas Eve, I want to go to the service at the church. Would you be interested in coming with me?"

Cody couldn't read the expression that crept over his dad's face.

"I'm going to have to pass on that, too, Cody."

"But, Dad—"

"Don't you dare question me on this. I'm not going to go into God's house out of habit or pretense. He took away the best thing in my life. He could have healed her, Cody, but he didn't. I begged him. But he did nothing. So God and I are done."

"You may think you're done with God, Dad. But he isn't done with you. He still loves you."

"He has a funny way of showing it."

"He gave you and Mom sixteen years together."

Cody saw his father's bottom lip begin to quiver. "That's not nearly enough. Was thirteen years enough for you, Cody? You happy how things have turned out?"

"No, of course not. But I'm thankful that I had a mom like her. I'm thankful for you. And I've been angry at God too. But in the end, I know he loves me. And I know he's wiser than I am. So I trust him."

"Well, you're just the model Christian, aren't you? You're a regular saint."

"Dad, please don't talk like that. I'm not a model anything. I miss her. I hurt just like you do. I wish she were still here."

Cody watched a tear track its way down his father's cheek.

"So do I, Son."

"Dad, please come to church with me on Christmas Eve."

"I've said no. It wouldn't be honest. At least I won't be a hypocrite like so many this time of year."

"But, Dad—you can go to church even if you're mad at God. Even if you're questioning him."

Cody's dad shook his head wearily. "Please, Cody—just let this go," he whispered.

"Okay, Dad. But I'll be praying for you. Please don't give up on God. He hasn't given up on us."

The phone rang, and Cody watched his dad run to answer it.

Cody frowned. He hadn't seen his father run to do anything in months. And he hadn't been inside a church since the funeral. He said he couldn't stand the looks of pity or the way people emphasized the word "are" when they asked, "How *are* you?"

But now Cody knew that Blake was right—there was more to it than that. Blake had suggested that Dad's heart was "clenched like a fist" because of the pain he was feeling. Cody stood in the hallway and listened to his father forcing a laugh as he talked on the phone.

Please, God, he prayed. *Open Dad's heart so your love can really touch it. And please don't be too angry at him for what he said. Amen.*

At 7:12 on Christmas morning, Cody opened his eyes and listened to the silence in the house. He propped

himself on one elbow and started to get out of bed, but grief was like a weight on his chest. He sank back onto the bed and closed his eyes.

Father God, he said quietly, *I know I should be happy today, but I'm just not. I'm sorry for that. The truth is, I've been dreading this—the first Christmas without her. I don't know how Dad and I are going to get through it. I'm so grateful that your Son came to earth. I really am. But this Christmas, I hope you'll forgive me if I can just be grateful but not happy.*

He opened his eyes again and stared at the ceiling. He drew in a deep breath and then wrinkled his nose. Did he smell a pie baking? It couldn't be. Dad barely knew how to operate the microwave. He'd heard of someone's eyes playing tricks on him, but could that happen with the nose too?

He sniffed. No, this was no smell mirage. A pie was baking. Either that or one of the fruit baskets had caught fire. He slipped out of bed and headed to the kitchen. The oven was on, and a pie sat on the middle rack. A Mrs. Smith's frozen-pie box was perched atop the overflowing garbage bin. Cody looked at the oven timer and saw twenty minutes remaining. Then he studied the instructions on the pie box and realized that Dad must have arisen at 6 a.m. to start the pie and bring some traditional Christmas aromatherapy to the Martin home.

Cody walked to the dining room and saw place settings for two. He shook his head.

God, he whispered, *there have been times I've felt like giving up hope on ever having a real dad again. Then he goes and pulls off something like this. Thanks. This has you written all over it.*

As Cody finished praying, his dad opened the front door, kicking his boots against each other to knock off the snow.

"Hey, Cody!" he said, too loudly, through a strained smile. He held out a small brown paper bag. "You wouldn't believe how hard it is to find someplace that's open on Christmas—and sells ice cream. Can't have apple pie without ice cream, right?"

Cody smiled. "Right, Dad."

After dinner, which consisted of reheated deli chicken, canned corn, and premade gelatin cubes, Cody and his father devoured the entire pie—except for one large piece they set aside for Pork Chop.

Then they exchanged presents. Cody gave his dad a cookbook called *Quick 'n' Healthy Recipes for the Man on the Go.* He knew Mom would approve. For years she had begged her husband to switch to a more healthful diet.

Cody had told the saleswoman that his dad wasn't exactly savvy in the kitchen, but she had assured him, "These recipes are super-duper easy. They're completely foolproof!"

"I guess we'll see," was Cody's reply.

Cody saw his dad forcing back tears as he held the book on his lap. "Thanks, Cody. This is the kinda gift she would have gotten me."

Then he handed Cody an Adidas shoebox, topped with an overly large red bow.

"I tried to wrap this at first," he explained. "But that really didn't go very well."

Cody nodded and lifted the lid. He inhaled the crisp smell of new leather and rubber—an aroma that rivaled even that of fresh-baked pie. He lifted the thin white tissue paper and revealed a pair of top-of-the-line mid-highs. Cody knew that Dad had probably dropped a C-note and a half on these shoes—and he didn't like to spend money.

"They're eight and a half," his Dad said. "I checked the other shoes in your closet, and most of them were that size. But we can take these back if they don't fit you. I thought your old shoes were looking a little beaten up. You're a good player. You deserve good shoes. The sales guy in the referee suit said they were the best."

"Thanks, Dad."

"You're welcome. Merry Christmas."

"Merry Christmas."

After watching the first half of the Lakers-Kings game on TV, Cody accompanied Blake to serve dinner at Mercy House. Dad had said he was too tired to come along. Cody had started to argue, but Blake nudged him with his elbow and whispered, "Let it go."

Mostly new faces greeted Cody as he served them, but he recognized a few individuals and families from years past. Mr. Thorne, whose cave-like mouth contained nine teeth—tops—nodded at Cody as he plopped a stiff mound of mashed potatoes on his tray.

"My condolences about your mom, young man. I miss her smile this Christmas."

Cody nodded back. "So do I."

Just before the volunteers began to put away the leftovers, Greta's family appeared. They stood in the doorway, Greta rubbing her bare hands together for warmth. Blake headed for them as if drawn by magnetic force.

"Welcome, Hopkins family!" he called. "You're just in time!"

Cody served Greta, her two younger brothers, and Mr. Hopkins and then untied his oversize white apron and hurried to the phone in the back room.

Five minutes later, Dad drove up, bearing the undersized gloves Cody's maternal grandma had mailed him from North Dakota. Dad also brought one of the superfluous fruit baskets.

Cody took the items and slid next to Greta at one of the long tables.

"This is for you and your family," he explained, putting the fruit basket next to her plate. "And these," he said, offering the gloves, "are just for you. So you don't get frostbite or something this winter."

"Thanks," Greta said, her voice almost a whisper. "I'm sorry I didn't get you anything. I, uh—"

Cody held his forefinger to his lips, realizing instantly that his mom used to do that. "It's cool, Greta. I don't need any presents. I'm just glad you're here."

Greta dipped her head. "Thanks. You know—for everything. If it weren't for you and Robyn—"

Cody smiled. "We got your back, Greta. You need anything, you just say so, okay?"

"Um, okay. Thanks. Again."

When cleanup was complete, Blake drove Cody home. Dad and Pork Chop were sitting together on the couch, the former looking on admirably as the latter attacked his piece of pie.

"Merry Christmas, dawg," Pork Chop said, crumbs tumbling from his mouth.

After exchanging gifts—a P.O.D. CD for Pork Chop and a "handsome rectangular green portrait of

Alexander Hamilton" for Cody—the duo shoveled the Martin driveway and shot baskets until dark.

"I wanted to wait 'til after Christmas to tell you the bad news," Coach Clayton told his team, at the first post-vacation practice. "Mister Alston has played his last basketball game for Grant Middle School."

Cody scanned the faces of his teammates. Their expressions ranged from puzzlement to shock.

"You recall Mister Alston's outburst in the Mill Creek game," Coach Clayton continued. "After that unfortunate episode, I spoke to him and required him to apologize to the official he yelled at, to you—his teammates—and to the principal. He refused. He won't play unless he says he's sorry, and it doesn't look like that's gonna happen."

"Man," Gannon whispered loudly to Cody, "we are toast."

Coach Clayton arched his eyebrows. "Is that so, Mister Gannon? We're toast? Does that mean you're quitting on us?"

Gannon chomped furiously on a wad of gum but said nothing.

"You see, Mister Gannon," Coach Clayton said, "I don't think we're toast. I think we're leading the conference. In fact, last time I checked, we're undefeated.

But if you think we're done, you can follow Terry Alston's lead and watch the rest of the season from the bleachers. That goes for anyone who has thoughts on giving up on our season. Just make sure you quit now. Don't do it out on the floor."

The coach walked over to where Gannon was sitting on the first row of bleachers and placed his hand on his head, as if he were going to bless him.

"Mister Gannon, I don't think you're a quitter. Hey—you're even starting to play some defense. So don't let all that tofu your mom feeds you go to your brain. I need you. I need all of you."

Coach Clayton moved Gannon to starting shooting guard for an away game with Cook. Gannon responded by playing out of his head. He hit half his shots for the first time in his life, scoring twelve points. He also dished out a career-high four assists. Grant won by fourteen.

That brought up Central. From the opening tip, Cody hounded Macy like a bill collector. Macy was scoreless until late in the first quarter, when he unveiled a new weapon. It was obvious to Cody that Macy had spent Christmas vacation working on an unblockable jump-hook. Despite Cody's nearly leaping out of his socks, he couldn't stop this new shot. Macy would finish the game with fourteen, but he wasn't Grant's biggest problem.

Clay did the real damage. He was simply too quick for Gannon, lighting him up for twenty-three points. Grant lost big, 42–23.

Macy didn't trash-talk much during the game, but after the final buzzer, he squeezed Cody's hand firmly as the teams congratulated each other at midcourt. Cody shuddered. There was something cold and reptilian about his grip.

"Remember this whupping, come districts, Martin," he sneered. "I've got your number now, and without Alston, you've got no chance."

"We'll see," Cody said, but he could tell his voice lacked confidence.

In the final two weeks of the regular season, Grant went 1–2, versus Maranatha, Lincoln, and Holy Family. Thus, the Raiders slipped to the third seed for districts.

"We're going to have to get by East to earn another crack at Central," Pork Chop moaned on the bus ride home from Holy Family. "And East is lookin' tough."

After the midweek pre-district practice, Cody stayed late to work on his free throws. After sinking seventy-three of one hundred shots, Cody shook his head in discouragement and headed for the showers. He almost collided with Alston in the locker room doorway.

"Watch where you're going, Martin," Alston mumbled.

Cody noted that Alston's words lacked the usual fire. It was as if he were reciting scripted lines in a bad high school play.

"Sorry, T," Cody said. "My bad."

"Whatever."

"Hey—what were you doing in the locker room?" Cody said hopefully. "Talking to Coach?"

"Yeah, right. Like I'm going to talk to him ever again. I just lost my stupid civics book. I thought it might be in my locker, but no such luck."

"You—you can borrow mine, if you want."

Alston's face showed genuine surprise. "What— you trying to make me feel bad or something?"

"No, I'm just trying to help—that's all."

Alston narrowed his eyes. "Why?"

"Because it's the right thing to do. And because we've been teammates. I wish we still were."

"Yeah, well—that ain't gonna happen."

"I guess not. But you can still borrow my book."

"What's your angle here, Martin? I don't get you."

Cody laughed softly. "Sometimes I don't get myself. Hey, hang on, okay?"

Cody rushed to his locker and returned with his battered copy of *Your World and You.*

Alston accepted the book with tentative hands.

"Thanks, Martin. But what about *you*?"

Cody smiled sheepishly. "I can probably get Robyn to study with me. Maybe Pork Chop, too, if I serve snacks."

Alston started to laugh, but then caught himself. "Well, thanks, Martin."

"No problem. But—T?"

"Yeah?"

"I'm not trying to tell you how to live your life or anything, but I wish you'd think about the whole apology thing. You're the best player in the league, maybe even the whole state. We need you."

"Look, Coach Clayton's a big—"

Cody held up his right hand, like a school crossing guard. "Please, I don't wanna hear it. Just think about what I said, okay?"

Alston ran a hand through his straw-colored hair. "Okay. Hey, Martin, does all this have anything to do with your being a Christian or whatever?"

Cody willed himself to meet Alston's eyes. "It pretty much has *everything* to do with that."

Alston nodded and walked away.

A couple of days later, Cody arrived for his morning free throws and saw Alston and Coach Clayton at the far end of the court, alternating jump shots.

Alston hit a baseline twenty-footer and jogged toward the locker room.

"Hey, you back on the team?" Cody asked as Alston moved by him.

"Yes and no," Alston said without turning around.

That night before warm-ups, the team sat in a half circle at midcourt. Alston, in street clothes, stood before them, rocking slowly from heels to toes.

"So I talked to Coach this morning," he began, "and I apologized to him for acting like a jerk against Creek. And I apologize to all of you too."

Alston looked to Coach Clayton, who gave him a parental nod.

"I will also apologize to that ref. It was a bad call, but we all make mistakes. I'm sorry if I embarrassed us as a team. And I wish I was still playing with you guys."

Cody and Pork Chop exchanged surprised expressions. Alston looked desperately uncomfortable, but he was saying all the right things.

"Anyway," Alston continued, "after I talked to Coach this morning, he said he'd take me back—as interim assistant coach. If it's okay with you guys."

Coach Clayton put his hand on Alston's shoulder. "So, fellas, what do you say?"

Cody cleared his throat and smiled at Alston. "Welcome back, Assistant Coach."

Pork Chop belched thoughtfully. "Yeah, welcome back, TA."

The others nodded their approval, and a smile of relief creased Alston's face.

During Grant's final two practices, Alston dove into his new role. He implored Gannon to square up on his jumpers, he worked with Goddard on his crossover dribble, and tutored Bart Evans on the art of the no-look pass.

Grant drew Holy Family in the first round of the district tourney. Cody heard Keenan Jones groan audibly the first time he picked up the Saint forward on defense. By the end of the first quarter, Cody had forced three bad passes, blocked a shot, and drawn two charging calls.

At the quarter break, Alston clapped Cody on the back.

"Martin, you are so inside of KJ's head. You've totally taken him out of his game!"

Jones hit his first basket two minutes before half-time, but by that point Grant was already up by twelve. On offense, the Raiders struggled to hit open jumpers, but Pork Chop and Brett Evans collected bushels of offensive rebounds and gave the team an array of second-chance hoops.

Holy Family made a last-minute run, but Pork Chop sealed the win with a three-point play. Final score— Grant 37, Holy Family 32.

The win brought up a semifinal matchup with Lincoln, who had upset East in the first round.

Before the game, Alston put his arm around Cody's shoulder.

"Cody, Locke is all these guys have. You shut him down, and this one is ours!"

Cody nodded. Alston needn't have said anything about Locke. But the speech did make an impression on him. It was the first time Alston had called him anything but "Martin" or something much worse.

Cody was relentless on Locke, fronting him every time he tried to post up in the low block. Miles, Lincoln's point guard, tried to force a few bullet passes, but Cody intercepted them or batted them away. And when Miles went to high lobs, they sailed over Locke's head and into Pork Chop's waiting hands—except for the two that hit the side of the backboard.

"That's the kind of defense that puts a smile on my big country face!" Coach Clayton said, praising Cody at halftime.

Cody collected his fourth foul with five minutes to go in the game as he battled with Locke for rebounding position. A minute later, he tried to block a Locke jumper and slapped him on the forearm instead.

Wearily, Cody jogged to the bench. Coach Clayton patted him on the head.

"Good game, dawg. You're gonna foul out once in a while when you play Monster D like that."

Cody slumped on the bench and watched Bart Evans, who replaced him in the lineup, front Locke on the low post.

"I had Bart watch you," Coach Clayton said. "I told him to do it exactly like you did."

Bart Evans wasn't as agile as Cody, but he was two inches taller, and Locke got only two touches for the remainder of the game. Grant won by thirteen, 41–28.

It was Grant and Central in the finals. Central won its first two games by twenty-eight and nineteen, respectively, with Macy scoring twenty-two and twenty-one.

As the teams positioned for the opening tip, Macy drew beside Cody.

"You're mine, Martin! You're gonna get rocked!"

Pork Chop planted himself on the other side of Macy, leaned in close to him, and belched in his ear.

"Rock that, Macy," he said.

Central controlled the opening tap, and Clay went immediately to Macy, who posted up Cody in the low block. Macy faked right and then pivoted left, elevated smoothly, and banked in a right-handed jump hook.

After Dylan tied the game with a baseline jumper, Central isolated Macy on Cody again. This time, Macy didn't go glass.

"Get used to it, boy," Macy said as the ball slid through the net.

After Macy hit his third straight shot over Cody, Coach Clayton called time-out. Alston met Cody before he got to the sidelines.

"Cody," he said, his voice already hoarse, "you gotta overplay Macy to his right hand. That way, you'll throw off his rhythm, force him to go lefty—and we both know he's got almost no game to his left. Come on, dude! You can shut him down!"

Coach Clayton joined the conversation. He handed Cody a water bottle.

"You understand what Terry's saying?"

Cody nodded slowly. "Yeah, yeah. I shoulda figured that out. I kinda lost my focus for a while. I'm sorry, Coach—I mean, coaches."

On Central's next possession, Macy found Cody nearly hanging on his right arm as he wheeled to shoot. Cody saw surprise in Macy's eyes as he launched his shot. The look went from surprise to dismay as the ball arced over the rim and into Dylan's hands.

Pork Chop fired an outlet pass to Goddard, then trailed Macy up the court, whispering loudly, "Air ball! Air ball!"

On Central's next two possessions, Clay shot free throw line jumpers, going one for two. Just before the end of the first quarter, Clay decided to give Macy another chance to get his jump-hook back on track. Again, Cody shaded Macy to his right—and leaped so hard he heard himself grunt as he strained to get at least a fingertip on Macy's shot.

Cody didn't touch any leather, but Macy left the shot short.

"Clank!" Pork Chop shouted as he grabbed the carom off the side of the rim.

Pork Chop winked at Cody as he set up on the high post.

"Get me the ball," he called.

Goddard swung the ball to Cody on the right wing. Cody immediately bounce-passed to Pork Chop, who backed deliberately toward the hoop, using his ample backside to push Miller, the Central postman, out of his way. Once he had Miller under the basket, Pork Chop stopped, elevated (a good three inches off the floor), and banked in a right-handed shot. The first quarter ended in a 14–14 deadlock.

The teams traded leads eleven times in the second quarter, with neither able to gain more than a three-point advantage. With one minute to go in the half, Macy came off of a high pick and tried to shake Cody with a series of head fakes, jukes, and jab steps. But Cody kept his center of gravity low and his body square with Macy's.

Cody heard Macy swear and then he dribbled to his right and launched an off-balance jumper. Cody leaped with him, straining to block the shot. Cody felt his middle finger brush the ball, but the shot still rattled in.

"Nice shot," Cody said.

Macy looked at him, suspicion creeping into his eyes. "What?"

"It was a good shot, that's all. I did all I could, and you still made it."

With that, Cody turned and trotted downcourt.

Brett Evans missed a runner in the lane. His brother snagged the rebound and cleared the ball to Dylan along the left baseline. Dylan drove to the hoop, but Clay cut him off. As Dylan searched in vain for some help, the halftime buzzer sounded.

Grant went to the locker room trailing by two, but Cody knew that the Raiders were still very much in the game.

In the visitors' locker room, the team sat attentively as Coach Clayton prepared to speak. Alston, who was sitting next to Cody, raised his hand.

"Coach, may I say something?"

Coach Clayton smiled cryptically.

"No, Terry—you may not."

Alston looked as if he had been stun gunned.

"Are you kidding me or something?"

"I never kid when it comes to basketball. You don't have time to talk, because you need to go see Dutch over at the entrance. He has your uniform."

Alston's jaw dropped. "But didn't you kick me off the team?"

"Not officially. See, Alston, I hoped you'd come around. You've shown me something as a coach. Now it's time to show me something as a player. I don't know what brought you around, but I'm sure glad it did."

Cody saw Alston look his way and nod once.

Alston entered the third quarter the way a starving man enters an all-you-can-eat buffet. He scored twelve points in eight minutes, six on fast breaks in which he simply outran the other nine players on the court.

Grant began the final quarter with a two-point lead. The margin grew to six after an Alston jumper from the foul line, then a reverse layup. Clay answered the latter with a fall-away jumper, but then Alston hit Dylan with a perfect behind-the-back pass on a two-on-one fast break.

Macy didn't even get to sniff the ball until two and a half minutes elapsed. He snared a high lob pass on the low post, but as he tried to back Cody under the backboard, he dribbled the ball off his foot.

At the quarter mid-point, the Raiders walked onto the court after a time-out.

"Man," said Brett Evans, staring at the scoreboard, which read Central 42, Visitor 48, "we might actually win this thing."

Dylan nodded in agreement. Cody wouldn't allow himself to nod, but he shared Dylan's hope.

Then Alston's game went up in smoke. Cody knew his teammate was in trouble when he saw him bent over, hands on knees, as he waited to shoot two free throws. Alston left both shots short.

Clay, noting Alston's fatigue, called for the ball. With a quick first step, he beat Alston to the baseline and hit an easy lay-in.

The next time down, Clay faked Alston into the air and earned a three-point play when he got slapped across the elbow on a jump shot.

As Alston jogged the ball upcourt, he raised his left hand like a surrender flag, signaling Coach Clayton to take him out of the game.

The coach called time-out and sent Gannon to the scorer's table. Alston collapsed on the bench, coughing like an old man.

"I'm sorry, Coach," he said, gasping for air. "I am worked!"

Coach Clayton nodded. "I take it you haven't stopped supporting the tobacco industry?"

Alston gave a guilty nod. "Well, I did think I was off the team. But I'll tell you right now—I'd like to find that Marlboro Man and Joe Camel and kick their sorry butts—no pun intended."

Coach Clayton smiled. "It's okay, TA. You've given us a chance to win—a chance we wouldn't have without you."

Then the coach addressed his team, "Okay, gentlemen. We're up three. We can win this. Sharp passes. Good shots. Tough defense. Martin, keep pressuring Macy full-court. If you keep taking him out of the offense, they are hurtin'. And Pork Chop, you keep gobbling up rebounds like the Cookie Monster gobbles up cookies, okay?"

Pork Chop nodded, his eyes meeting Cody's. The Raiders stacked their hands on Coach Clayton's.

"Let's hear 'defense' on three," he said.

"Defense!" the team called in near-perfect unison. Before moving on court, Cody looked up in the stands, behind the team bench, and found Blake and his dad. Dad nodded. Blake made a fist with his right hand and pounded it against his chest.

Robyn, who was sitting with Greta, behind Blake, simply pointed at Cody and smiled. He wasn't sure what she meant, but he felt energized nonetheless.

Dylan inbounded the ball to Cody. He turned and saw Macy giving him room. He squared up and launched a jump shot from eighteen feet, barely in his range. He thought he had left the shot short, but the ball nudged the side of the rim and then crept over for two.

As he sprinted back on defense, Cody risked a look to the stands. He saw Blake pounding Dad's back as both stood to roar their approval.

Cody's moment of inattention allowed Macy to get free for a jumper from the left baseline. Fortunately, Macy lost control of the ball as he went up and had to adjust his shot in midair. The hesitation was all Cody needed to recover. He charged, not directly at Macy, but to a spot two feet in front of him. As he propelled his body upward, he knew he was finally going to get a real block, not just a deflection.

Macy followed his shot to the basket, but the ball wasn't going to make it to the basket. Cody redirected it back over Macy's head and right to Bart Evans.

Grant got a good shot on their next offensive set, but Goddard missed a five-foot bank shot in the lane. Macy out-jumped Pork Chop for the rebound and caught Clay streaking downcourt for an uncontested layup.

After a Brett Evans miss, Clay pulled Central even with Grant as he hit a layup, drew a foul on Goddard, and converted the three-point play.

With thirty seconds left in the game, Gannon walked the ball up court. As he crossed the midcourt stripe, Clay and Macy trapped him. Gannon tried a desperation baseball pass across court to Goddard but threw it over his head.

Cody thought Central would call time-out, but Clay quickly inbounded the ball to Macy, who gave it right back to his teammate. Cody clenched his teeth as he saw Central isolate Clay against Goddard. Clay had three inches on Goddard—and probably three seconds in the 100-yard dash. He thought about leaving Macy to help out his teammate, but he couldn't risk leaving the league's best clutch shooter open.

Goddard did everything he could to stay with Clay, but when the latter drove hard to the hoop, stopped abruptly, and elevated for a fallaway jumpshot, there was nothing to do but watch as Central pulled ahead by two, with nine seconds left in the game.

"No time-outs! No time-outs left," Coach Clayton bellowed from the sidelines.

Gannon nodded as he looked to inbound the ball. Clay pressured Goddard as he tried to free himself in the backcourt.

Cody could see Gannon straining to find an open man. Dylan dashed into the backcourt, Macy on his heels. Gannon's eyes locked on Dylan as he fired a chest pass in his direction.

Gannon's pass sailed toward midcourt. Dylan and Macy both lunged for it. Dylan got his fingertips on the ball, but he couldn't control it. It glanced off his right hand and went out of bounds.

"White ball!" the lead referee yelled.

Quickly, Clay moved to the referee's side and waited for the ball. Cody nodded grimly.

No time-out again, eh? Good strategy, with only six seconds remaining, but this time I'm ready.

He attached himself to Macy like a barnacle. He felt certain Clay would go to the player with the best hands. Then again, that would be predictable. Maybe Macy would just be a decoy. *What was Clay thinking?*

Cody knew the answer when he felt Macy push him hard in the back. It should have been a foul, but that was okay. This was almost as good. Clay and

Macy had tipped their hand. They probably practiced this stunt a thousand times. Push the defender to get separation, and then catch the high-lob pass.

Cody pretended to stumble forward as Macy sprinted away from him. Clay unleashed a high, arcing pass. Cody regained the balance that he had never really lost and closed the gap between himself and Macy.

As Cody spring-loaded himself to leap and intercept the ball, he tried to calculate how much time the Raiders would have to score—probably five seconds, if he could snag Clay's pass.

The "if" quickly became reality. Cody snared the ball with his right hand. He took two dribbles upcourt.

Five, four . . . he counted to himself.

He saw Pork Chop break free at center court. He rocketed a chest pass to him. Pork Chop turned and dribbled toward the top of the key. Cody broke for the basket. He wasn't sure there would even be time for a rebound and a put-back, but this wasn't something you left to chance.

Three, two . . .

Pork Chop stopped just inside the top of the key and went up for a jumper. Macy was right on him, and Clay charged in at the last second to get a hand in his face too.

Pork Chop's shot hit the back of the rim and bounced high into the air. Goddard tipped the rebound away from Macy and controlled the ball along the left perimeter of the lane. He had just elevated for a jump shot when the final buzzer blared.

Cody saw the lead ref waving off the shot before Goddard released and swished it.

Goddard must have seen the ref, too, because he collapsed to his knees, covering his face with both hands. Pork Chop knelt beside him, wrapping a sweaty arm around his teammate.

Cody stood before Goddard and Pork Chop. It looked as if they were both crying. But Pork Chop was sweating so profusely that it was hard to tell.

Cody extended both hands. "It's okay, guys. We gave it all we had."

Goddard and Pork Chop each took a hand, and Cody yanked them to their feet. Where he found the strength to do it, he wasn't sure. As the threesome walked to the bench, Cody surveyed the bleachers. Nearly everyone was standing, and they were all applauding.

"Ladies and gentlemen," the public address announcer said, "we ask that you stay in your seats for the presentation of the trophies and the announcement of the all-district tournament team—and this year's tournament MVP."

When the Raiders went to center court to accept the runner-up trophy, Central's athletic director handed it to Pork Chop.

"You are a warrior, big man," he said.

"We *all* are, sir," Pork Chop said, handing the trophy to Goddard.

After watching Central accept the championship trophy, Cody leaned toward Pork Chop.

"I hope you made all-tourney, Chop. You deserve it."

"Thanks," Pork Chop said, finishing off a cup of Gatorade and belching.

The first two all-tournament selections were no surprise. Mike Riley was a hard-nosed player who made few mistakes. And Bobby Cabrera had been spectacular, even though he couldn't carry his team to the finals. He scored twenty-five in the opening game.

"R-r-r-r-r-rick Macy!" the PA announcer called, drawing whoops of approval from the hometown crowd. Macy walked slowly to center court, where he accepted his medal and shook hands with Cabrera and Riley.

Come on, Cody said to himself. *Call Chop's name. Come on!*

"Cody Martin, of the Grant Raiders!" said the announcer, with about half the gusto and volume that he gave Macy.

Cody sat stunned on the Raider bench. He looked to Coach Clayton, who said, "Every dawg has his day!" Cody felt hands pounding on his back as he rose slowly to his feet. He heard ferocious barking and knew it was coming from Pork Chop and the Evans twins.

Riley offered his hand as Cody stood beside him, and Macy leaned in his direction and shouted over the applause, "Good tournament, Martin. I have a feeling we're going to be seeing a lot of each other in high school."

Cody nodded. He looked down the line at Cabrera, who was staring straight ahead.

"Whatever," Cody said quietly.

When one of Central's cheerleaders placed the medal around his neck, Cody closed his eyes for a moment. Then he tilted his head up and pointed both index fingers to the sky.

In the stands, Greta tapped Robyn on the shoulder, tears gleaming in her eyes. "Do you think he's pointing up at his mom, or at God?" she asked.

Robyn smiled, "Probably at both of them. They're up there together—you know? And I have a feeling they're both smiling big-time right now."

There wasn't much mystery about all-star number five. Antwan Clay was clearly the best player in the tournament, and now he had a medal and an MVP trophy to prove it.

Clay chest-bumped Macy and then took his place beside Cody as the quintet smiled for pictures. Between shots, Clay leaned in to Cody.

"Nice defense, dawg. If it weren't for you, Macy might be holding this trophy right now."

When Cody emerged from the locker room, his dad was waiting for him. He placed both hands on Cody's shoulders. "You know what your mom always said about you—as an athlete, I mean?"

"Uh, no, I guess not."

"She always told me you were gallant. Interesting word, huh? I never really knew what she meant. I guess I didn't watch you enough to know. But after tonight, Cody, I know."

"Thanks, Dad." Cody said, leaning into his dad as he put his arm around him.

On the Monday after the tournament, Terry Alston caught up with Cody in the hallway and grabbed him by the elbow.

"Cody," he said, "I just want you to know that I had nothing to do with it. Nothing at all. I can't really tell you who did it, but it's not someone who's a student here. It's not Neale, so don't bring the war on him, okay?"

Cody didn't even have time to say "Huh?" before Alston turned and jogged away.

Cody didn't find out what the "it" was until Robyn approached him at lunch and led him to Greta's locker.

In red marker, someone had scrawled "DEATH TO GUT-BUCKET GRETA!"

"Did she see this?" Cody asked.

"It's her locker," Robyn said quietly, just before she buried her face in her hands and began crying quietly.

Tentatively, Cody laid his hand on her shoulder.

"I tried so hard, Cody," she said. "I tried so hard to stop it. I thought it was over."

Cody tried to find Greta several times during the day. Finally he went to Mr. Prentiss's office, where he learned that Greta had gone home early.

He suggested to Robyn that they visit the bus-house that afternoon, but she convinced him to "give Greta a little space and let's talk to her tomorrow."

But Greta didn't come to school the next day. Robyn told Cody that she would check on her that evening, but that she wanted to do it alone.

On Wednesday, neither Robyn nor Greta came to school. Cody called the Hart house twice that evening but got the answering machine both times.

On Thursday morning, Robyn was waiting at Cody's locker when he arrived at school. She smiled at him, but it was a sad smile.

"Come with me," she said softly.

She led him to the Home Ec room, where a large platter of chocolate chip cookies sat on Ms. Young's desk. They were covered with green cellophane. An envelope with CODY, written in large block letters, lay beside the cookies.

"Read it," Robyn said.

Carefully, Cody tore open the envelope and removed a folded page of notebook paper. Somehow, even before he read the letter, he knew it was from Greta.

Dear Cody,

My family and I have decided to move. It is just too hard for me at Grant. My dad has a job possibility in Tennessee, and it's warmer there. Which is nice, since winter's here.

I won't miss much about Grant, but I will miss you and Robyn. Thank you for being my friends and for standing up for me. No one outside my family has ever done that for me.

I hope you like the cookies. It's your mom's recipe. Robyn got it from your dad. I'm sure they won't be as good as your mom's, but I did my best. I even stole some real butter, since all Ms. Young had was margarine. Please ask God to forgive me. Maybe someday I can pay the store back.

Also, I want to tell you that you are a great athlete. I am proud of how you played in the tournament. I watched almost all of your home games this year. I don't think you saw me most of the time, but I was there. But even though you are a great athlete,

*you are an even better friend. And that is how I will
always think of you. As my friend.*

*God bless,
Greta Hopkins*

Cody swallowed hard and looked at Robyn. "What
do we do now, Hart?"

"I think we say a silent prayer for Greta and her
family," she said. "Then we have a cookie."

Cody closed his eyes and listened to the hollow echo
of leather on hardwood as he dribbled the ball slowly
at the free throw line of the empty Grant gym. He
knew Coach Clayton would be in soon to lock up. He
squared up and swished a free throw. Then he walked
slowly to retrieve the ball as it rolled to a stop against
the back wall.

"Good shootin', dawg."

Cody looked at Coach Clayton, his lanky body
framed by the doorway.

"Thanks, Coach," he said. "And I mean thanks for
everything."

"Thank *you*. You played like a sure-enough warrior
this year."

Cody held the ball against his hip. "I'm gonna miss
this game," he said.

"You gonna be okay, Martin? You seem really down."

"It's just sad the season's over. And one of my friends moved away. I guess I'm kinda sad about that too."

Coach Clayton nodded slowly. "Yeah. I heard about that. But there are times when life is like basketball. You do all you can, but you can't really control the final outcome. I guess that's in bigger hands than ours, you know?"

"Yeah, but it's still hard."

"Well," the coach said, cupping a hand around the back of Cody's neck and steering him toward the exit, "I wish there was something I could do to cheer you up."

Cody looked up at his coach. "Maybe there is."

"And what would that be?"

"Just tell me that it won't be too long before track starts."

Coach Clayton laughed. "It'll be here before you know it. But do you really think you can be a track man? You're not the fastest guy in the world, you know."

"I know. But Blake said something on Sunday that gives me hope. He said that the race isn't always to the swiftest. Sometimes the guy who wins is the one who just keeps on running."

"I'll buy that," the coach said, smiling. "Hey, you need a ride home? Or change to call your old man?"

"Nah, I think I'll run home."

"I'm not sure that's such a good idea, dawg. I just chased that moron Gabe Weitz outta the lobby a few minutes ago. I know all about him, you know. Mr. Porter told me. You two better watch your backs."

"We will, Coach. Doug says that if we can steer clear of him until graduation, our troubles will be over."

Coach Clayton smiled. "Yes, it would be bad to get kicked out of school before graduation. That might ruin one's full-ride football scholarship."

"But once Doug graduates, he says that he and Weitz are going to have 'a conversation.'"

Coach Clayton frowned. "I don't want to hear any more about any of that. The less I know, the better. I told Mr. Weitz that I would be keeping an eye on him, but he didn't look worried. I think you should let me drive you home. It's cold anyway. Running home would be—"

"Gallant. That's what it is, Coach."

Coach Clayton smiled. "Gallant—I like that word."

"So do I."

With that, Cody tucked his ball under his arm and sprinted for the exit. The only vehicles he saw on the way were parked, slumbering under thick blankets of snow.

Cody felt the grain of the leather on his fingertips. He turned his prize possession over and over in his hands.

"You've meant a lot to me, especially this season," he said quietly.

It felt a bit strange, talking to an inanimate object, but then again, he didn't truly regard the Bible as lifeless.

He opened his Bible and turned to the inscription. It read,

> *Cody,*
>
> *Know always that you are loved. You have his Word on that.*
>
> > *Love,*
> > *Mom and Dad*
> > *Christmas 2003*

Cody nodded and then turned the pages toward the Psalms. That's what he felt like reading right now—a psalm in which David slam-dunked his fears and insecurities and praised God for the challenges, the excitement, and the pure joy of simply being alive.

SPIRIT OF THE GAME

Cody's determined to finish the race, no matter what!

SECOND WIND

BY TODD HAFER

ZONDERVAN

Chapter 1
Men Versus Mountain

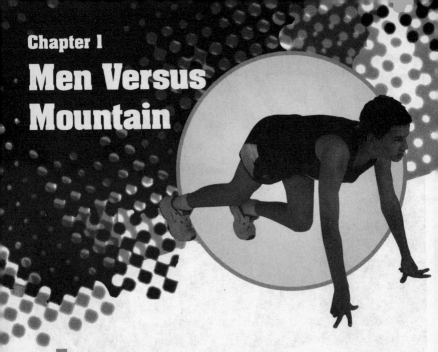

"This is way worse than running suicides, Martin," Bart Evans groaned. "This is the kind of thing that could kill a guy for real! Dude, I thought he was tough as a hoops coach. But this is, like, another level of pain."

Eighth grader Cody Martin nodded grimly. *I'd rather run a hundred suicides than do this*, he thought. *Why did I let Coach Clayton talk me into this?* He rose up from his saddle as the road steepened. Each downstroke on the pedals of his 12-speed felt as if it would be his last. His quads burned, like they had been soaked in acid.

"If I peddle any slower," he mumbled, "I'll start going back downhill. I can't believe Coach made this sound fun."

Bart snorted weakly. "Coach Clayton is the devil. 'Scenic ride,' my foot, which is aching so bad I want to cut it off, by the way. 'Majestic ride, carving right through a historic Colorado mountain pass. Breathtaking rock walls so close to the road's edge you can reach out and touch them.'"

"Well," Cody offered, "it would be scenic, if we weren't blinded by pain."

The duo grew silent as they rounded a switchback and were hit by a stiff wind.

I should have suspected something when Coach Clayton dodged Gage's question, Cody thought. Gage McClintock, the track team's best 400-meter runner, had asked the distance coach, "Mountain pass, eh? I don't like the sound of that. How steep a mountain are we talkin' here?"

Coach Clayton, a six-foot-four scarecrow of a man, had laughed derisively. "Mac, don't be such a wimp. It's only a fourteen-mile ride. We're not talking about a leg of the Tour de stinkin' France. Not even a toe of the Tour de France. For cryin' out loud, I'm doin' the ride on my old mountain bike. You guys all have road bikes, so quit your whinin'."

"Besides," he added with a wink, "when we finish up in Woodland Park, I'm gonna buy you the best donuts anywhere. And then we get to ride *down*. I'm tellin' ya—you'll feel like you're flyin'!"

Flyin'? Cody thought. *A snail could crawl faster than this. I'm gonna topple over any second now, I just know it. It's just a matter of physics. It's not possible for a bike to go this slow.*

Cody knew that if he crashed, he was going to leave significant portions of his hide on Ute Pass. His cycling shoes were locked firmly in the toe clips, and he wouldn't have the time or energy to release them, especially if he biffed when he was up off the saddle. He raised his head to study the terrain ahead. His heart deflated like a balloon. Just ahead was the meanest hill of the ride.

It has to be two hundred yards long, Cody thought. *And it's straight up, no switchbacks!*

He heard himself whimper. Bart had pulled ten yards ahead of him moments earlier, but now Cody saw him maneuver his bike off the shoulder and execute an ungainly dismount. As he stood on the roadside, his legs buckled, and he had to lean on his bike for support.

Softcover 0-310-70670-X

Available now at your local bookstore!

ZONDERVAN®

We want to hear from you. Please send your comments about this book to us in care of zreview@zondervan.com. Thank you.

GRAND RAPIDS, MICHIGAN 49530 USA